검은방

검은 방
The Black Room

정지아 | 손정인 옮김
Written by Jeong Jeong Ji-a
Translated by Sohn Jung-in

K

ASIA
PUBLISHERS

차례

Contents

검은 방
The Black Room

창문을 블라인드로 가려도 빛은 어디론가 새어든다. 강 건너 도로를 질주하는 차 소리가 잦아들고 사위가 적막에 감싸이기 시작하면 빛의 자리를 어둠이 슬금슬금 잠식한다. 그제야 아흔아홉 해 혹사당한 그녀의 눈에 생기가 돈다. 어둠의 가운데 놓여 있을 때 그녀의 몸도 비로소 이완된다. 수십 년 버텨오는 동안 생겨난 장롱의 흠집이나 가구 사이사이 뭉친 먼지 같은 것들도 이제는 어둠에 가려 보이지 않고, 제 흔적마저 까맣게 지워, 검은 방에는 오직 그녀와 어둠뿐이다. 산골의 밤은 방해할 무엇도 없어 태초의 어둠 그 자체다. 태초에 어둠이 있었다. 하나의 정자가 어둠을 건너 어둠 속에

Light comes into the room somehow, even with the window shade down. When the traffic sound from the road across the river dies down, absolute silence begins to fill everywhere, and darkness stealthily encroaches on the realm of light. Only then do her eyes, which have been exploited for ninety-nine years, begin to twinkle. Only in the midst of darkness does her body relax at last. Scratches on her decades-old armoire and dust balls under the furniture are now invisible in the dark, leaving no trace at all, and only she and darkness exist in the black room. Free from any interruption, the night in the mountain village is primal darkness itself. In the beginning was darkness. A sperm crossed darkness to meet an

웅크린 난자를 만났다. 수정과 세포분열 또한 어둠 속에서 은밀하게 행해졌다. 어머니의 자궁 속에서 보낸 열 달 동안 그녀는 대체로 눈을 뜨지 못했고 무심코 눈을 뜬 어떤 날, 얇아질 대로 얇아진 어머니의 뱃가죽 사이로 스며든 희미한 빛이 눈을 찔러 황급히 눈을 감았다. 처음 대면한 빛은 통증이었다. 눈이 빛을 받아들이고 환한 빛 속에서 사물을 인식할 수 있을 때까지 몇 달의 시간이 걸렸다. 빛과 어둠의 순환 속에서 그녀는 아흔아홉 해를 살았다.

눈을 뜬들 감은들 보이는 것은 어둠뿐, 그녀는 차라리 눈을 감는다. 눈을 감자 비로소 빛 속에서 보이지 않던 것들이 보인다. 그것은 때로 기억의 한 조각이기도 하고, 꿈의 한 조각이기도 하다. 갓 서른의 그녀가 수의를 짓고 있다. 가회에서 죽은 박종하의 수의다. 박종하는 남편의 절친한 친구였고, 일찍 산에서 죽은 남편을 대신해 그녀를 살뜰하게 챙겨준 그녀의 친구기도 했다.

금방 댕겨올라요.

불과 두 시간 전, 박종하는 희디흰 얼굴에 피부색보다 더 밝은 웃음을 짓고 임시로 묵고 있던 집을 나섰다. 잠시 뒤 소복을 입은 한 어린 처자가 조심조심 발소리 죽

egg crouching in the dark. Insemination and cell division also occurred secretly in the dark. During the ten months in her mother's womb, she stayed mostly with her eyes closed, and when she opened her eyes by chance one day, she hastily closed them again, blinded by a ray of dim light coming through the thinnest belly skin of her mother. The first light she faced was pain. It took a few months of time for her eyes to receive light and to perceive things in bright light. In cycles of light and darkness, she has lived ninety-nine years.

Whether open or closed, her eyes can see only darkness, so she prefers to keep them closed. With her eyes closed, she can finally see things that had been invisible in light. It is a piece of memory sometimes, and a piece of dream at other times. At the tender age of thirty, she is sewing a shroud. It is for Pak Jong-ha who died in Gahoe. Pak was a close friend of her husband and also a friend of hers, who took sincere care of her on behalf of her deceased husband who had died an untimely death in the mountains.

"I'll be back soon."

Only two hours ago, Pak left his temporary home with a smile brighter than his fair skin. A little later, a young woman in white mourning clothes followed him carefully on tiptoe. Her policeman husband had been killed at the Anui police substation during the

여 박종하의 뒤를 밟았다. 며칠 전 남부군의 안의지서 습격 때 순경이었던 남편을 잃은 처자였다. 어린 처자의 가슴에 남편 잃은 슬픔이 번질 새도 없이 희고 잘난 박종하의 얼굴이 들어찼다. 어린 처자는 소복을 입은 채 소복보다 처연한 얼굴로 남부군의 행렬 맨 뒤를 따랐다. 다 죽을 운명인지도 모르고 자신들의 묘지 지리산을 향해 남하하는 남부군은 백전백승, 사기 충만했다. 박종하는 그 남부군의 전투사령관이었다. 박종하는 가회에 당도한 후에야 자기 총알에 맞아 죽었을지도 모르는 순경의 아내가 자기를 따라왔다는 사실을 알았다.

아짐씨, 이것은 아니지라. 이것은 인두껍을 쓰고 사램이 헐 짓이 아니지라. 가써요. 존 일에 후딱 가써요이.

어린 처자는 처연한 얼굴로 뚝뚝 동백꽃 같은 눈물만 흘렸다. 소복을 입은 채 남편 죽인 남자에게 빠져 뒤를 밟아온 여자의 눈물은 어떤 의미였을까. 부끄러움이었을까, 죄책감이었을까. 부끄러움도 죄책감도 활활 태워버린 사랑이었을까. 뚝뚝 눈물만 떨구며 여자는 꿈쩍도 하지 않았다. 지켜보던 박종하가 노여운 얼굴로 쾅쾅 발을 굴렀다. 어쩌지 못해 여자가 뒤돌아섰다. 박종하도 매정하게 돌아섰다. 다시 돌아선 여자는 뒤도 돌아

attack by partisan troops of the Southern Army[1] a few days before. Pak's fair and handsome looks had enchanted her before she felt grief over her husband's death. The young woman walked behind the partisan procession in white mourning clothes with a face paler than clothes. Not knowing their doomed fate, the unbeaten Southern Army marched south toward Jirisan Mountain with high morale, which would be their burial ground. Pak was the combat commander of the Army. Not until he arrived at Gahoe did he realize that the widow of a policeman who might have been killed by his bullet was following him.

"Ma'am, this ain't right. This is not a human thing to do. Go away! Go right away!"

Teardrops fell from the young woman's pale face, like falling camellias. What could be the meaning of tears shed by a woman in mourning clothes, who fell for and followed a man that had killed her husband? Was it shame? Or was it a sense of guilt? Or was it love that burnt both shame and the sense of guilt into ashes? The young woman, not moving at all, just shed teardrops. Watching her, Pak made an angry face and stamped his foot loudly on the ground. She was compelled to turn around. He also

1) The Southern Army refers to communist partisans of the North Korean Army operating in South Korea.

보지 않고 성큼성큼 걸어가는 박종하의 뒷모습을, 첫걸음 뗀 제 아이 보듯, 세상에 다시없는 다정한 눈길로 더듬고 어루만졌다. 칡꽃 향기 끈적끈적, 맨살에 엉겨 붙던 여름날이었다.

그러고도 여자는 떠나지 않았다. 어디서 밤을 보낸 건지 박종하가 머물던 집 부근을 서성이다 다음날, 박종하의 뒤를 밟은 것이다. 금방 댕겨온다던 박종하는 여느 때처럼 총알이 빗발치는 전장에서 허리를 꼿꼿이 세운 채 싸우다 못 된 총알 한 방에 심장을 관통당해 즉사했다, 고 누군가 울면서 전했다. 그녀는 울지 않았다.

먼저 가 계시씨요. 금방 따라 갈라요.

눈물 한 방울 없이 남편을 보내고, 박종하를 보내고, 이현상도 보냈다. 금방 따라갈 줄 알았다. 금방이 십 년이 되고 이십 년이 되고, 칠십 년이 될 줄은 꿈에도 몰랐다. 아흔아홉이 된 지금, 그녀는 오래도록 잊고 있었던 기억인지, 긴 시간이 만들어낸 기억의 왜곡인지, 혹은 늙어 헛것을 보는 것인지, 수의 짓는 그녀 옆에서 목 놓아 통곡하는 젊은 처자의 얼굴을 선명하게 떠올린다. 양 볼에 홍조가 있고, 그 위로 주근깨가 오종종 깨알처럼 박혀 있다. 스물이나 되었을까. 여자는 제 남편이 죽

turned around mercilessly. She turned about again and stared at his back as he strode away and did not look back, touching and caressing him with her eyes with unparalleled affection, as if watching her child taking its first step. It was a summer day when the heavy scent of kudzu flowers stuck to bare skin.

Even then, the young woman would not leave. Having spent the night hovering around Pak's temporary home, the woman followed him again the next day. Having promised to come back soon, Pak fought with his back straight as usual on the battlefield in a hail of bullets, but was killed instantly by an evil bullet piercing right through his heart. Thus said a weeping witness. She did not cry.

"You go first. I will follow you soon."

She had survived her husband, Pak Jong-ha and Yi Hyeon-sang[2] without shedding a tear. She expected to follow them soon. Never did she dream that ten years, twenty years and seventy years would roll by so soon. Now at the age of ninety-nine, she recalls a clear image of the face of the wailing young woman sitting beside her while she was sewing a shroud, whether it is a long-forgotten memory, or a distorted memory caused

2) Yi Hyeon-sang was the commander-in-chief of the Southern Army during the Korean War.

었을 때보다 더 섧게 목 놓아 흐느낀다. 온 마음을 사로잡아 지옥불도 뛰어넘게 만드는, 그, 사랑이라는 것일까. 그런 사랑을 아흔아홉 해, 여우가 꼬리 아홉 달린 불여우로 둔갑하고도 남을 세월을 살아오는 동안, 그녀는 경험해본 적이 없다. 아니, 그보다 더 뜨거운 사상이라는 것을 가슴에 품고 지옥불을 건너오기는 했다. 이것과 그것은 같은 것일까, 다른 것일까.

수의를 짓는 서른의 그녀는 사랑 따위에 마음을 뺏겨, 고작 몇 번 보지도 않은 남자의 죽음 앞에서 오열하는 젊은 처자를, 그 처자의 어리고 여윈 어깨 위로 쏟아지는 뜨거운 햇살까지 얼릴 듯한 차가운 눈빛으로 경멸하고 있다. 살아도 살아도 모르겠는 세상, 그러지 말 것을, 서러운 등짝 한 번 가만히 쓸어줄 것을, 그 가만한 손길로 어쩌면 여자는 사랑에 미친 제 죄를 용서받은 양, 한평생 견뎌냈을지도 모를 것을…….

그러나 서른의 그녀는 퍼렇게 날 선 한 자루 검이었다. 보듬는 것보다 베는 것이 더 산뜻했다. 나흘이나 쌀한 톨 먹지 못한 채 차가운 동굴의 물속에 몸을 숨기고 있을 때, 코앞으로 지나가는 국군의 무리를 피해 숨을 죽일 때, 미군의 총탄이 그녀의 정수리에 가르마를 남기

by the long time, or an apparition caused by her old age. The young woman has rosy cheeks peppered with freckles. The woman is twenty years old at most, wailing for Pak more bitterly than for her own husband. Can it be the true love that captivates your heart and makes you jump over the hellfire? Never has she experienced that kind of love in her whole life of ninety-nine years, which is a long enough time for a fox to change into a nine-tailed vixen. Indeed, she has also jumped over the hellfire to embrace something more passionate than that-an ideology. Is this the same as that, or different?

While sewing a shroud at the age of thirty, she despises the young woman who is captured by such a trivial thing as love and wailing for a man whom she has seen only a few times, and stares at the woman with steely eyes that can freeze the hot sunlight pouring onto the woman's little skinny shoulders. The world remains incomprehensible no matter how long she lives, so she should not have done it, but instead, should have gently patted the grieving woman on the back. Her gentle hands could have helped the woman endure life, as if she had been forgiven of her sin of falling crazy in love. . .

At the age of thirty, however, she was a sharp-bladed sword. Cutting seemed fresher than

며 스쳐 지날 때, 그녀는 머리카락 한 올의 떨림까지, 피 톨의 성난 움직임까지 감각할 수 있었고, 그런 것이 살 아있는 것이라 믿었다. 명료하고 산뜻하게 살다 목숨 따 위 사상을 위해 명료하고 산뜻하게 버리려 했다. 그러나 그녀는 살아남았고, 어느 순간, 산에서의 날 선 감각은 동지섣달 아랫목의 갱엿처럼 흐물흐물 녹아내렸다.

리모컨 전원 버튼을 누른 듯 서른의 그녀가 순식간에 사라지고, 그녀는 아흔아홉의 노파가 된다. 그녀는 블 라인드 사이로 스며드는, 빛이라기에는 너무 희미해 빛 과 어둠의 경계와 같은, 묽은 어둠을 향해 굼뜨게 몸을 움직인다. 블라인드를 들추자 깊은 어둠 저편, 불 밝힌 방 하나가 등대처럼 둥실 어둠 속에 떠 있다. 그녀의 날 선 감각을 갱엿처럼 녹인 딸아이의 집이다. 아흔아홉 해의 긴 생은 딸 덕분이기도 했다.

산에서 붙잡힌 그녀는 오 년간 감옥살이를 했다. 다시 마주한 세상은 너도 나도 친일청산을 외치고 조국 통일 을 외치던 해방 직후와 전혀 달랐다. 그녀가 목숨 바쳐 지키려 했던 그것들을 이제는 아무도 입에 올리지 않았 다. 빨갱이인 그녀는 더더욱 그런 말을 입에 올릴 수 없 었다. 침묵의 세월을 견디는 동안 기억만이 그녀의 편

embracing to her. When hiding in a cold watery cave without eating a grain of rice for four days, when holding her breath to avoid a bunch of ROK soldiers marching right in front of her, and when narrowly escaping a US bullet that whizzed past her to part her hair, she could feel the bristling of her hair and even the angry movements of her red blood cells. That was the way to live, she believed. She wanted to live a lucid and fresh life, and to sacrifice it in a lucid and fresh way for the sake of her ideology. She survived, however, and at a certain point, her sharp-edged sense of life in the mountains melted down like a piece of mushy taffy on a hot floor in midwinter.

As if pressing the power button on the remote control, the thirty-year old disappears in a flash, and she becomes a ninety-nine-year-old woman. She slowly moves toward a feeble light coming through the shade, or rather toward a feeble darkness, since the light is so dim that it is on the border between light and darkness. She lifts the shade, and beyond deep darkness, sees a lighted window floating in the dark like a lighthouse. It is her daughter's place, who has melted her sharp-edged sense of life like mushy taffy. She owes her long life of ninety-nine years to her daughter.

After being captured in the mountains, she was locked behind bars for five years. She returned to

이었다. 48년 12월부터 54년 1월까지, 한순간도 잊히지 않고 갈수록 생생해지는 기억보다 더 괴로운 것은 남정네들의 욕정이었다. 남편조차 없는 서른 중반의 빨갱이년 따위, 어떻게 해도 상관없는 시대였다. 자식 일곱 딸린 쉰 넘은 홀아비의 청혼은 기본이요, 평소 누나라며 따르던, 사촌동생의 친구가 늦은 밤 월담을 해 덮치려한 적도 있었다. 어린 학생 녀석의 휘파람 같은 건 애교였다. 산에서 그녀는, 혁명가요, 동지였다. 아무도 그녀를 한낱 여자로 대하지 않았다. 산에서 죽었어야 한다고, 그녀는 날마다 피가 나도록 입술을 깨물었다. 죽지 못해 남자들의 욕정 앞에 먹잇감으로나 내던져진 제 몸뚱이를 그녀는 도무지 용서할 수가 없었다.

그 무렵, 한 남자가 찾아왔다. 전 남편과 박종하의 친구이자 동지였다. 그는 긴 감옥살이를 끝내고 막 세상으로 돌아온 참이었다.

빨갱이 둘이 같이 있는 걸 남이 봐 좋을 리 없다 생각한 것인지 그는 둘 다 가르친 바 있는 은사의 집으로 그녀를 불렀다. 늙은 선생이 대문간에서 망을 보고 문 닫힌 안방에 둘은 마주 앉았다. 할 말이 태산 같을 줄 알았는데 막상 말이 나오지 않았다. 태산 같은 마음을 어떤

society totally different from what it used to be immediately after the liberation of Korea, when everyone had called for the punishment of pro-Japanese Koreans and reunification. No one mentioned those things for which she had risked her life anymore. On top of that, being a 'commie,' she did not dare to mention them. While she withstood the test of time in silence, memory was the only thing that was on her side. She was distressed by her clear memories from December 1948 to January 1954 which were not forgotten for a minute but becoming more vivid as years went by, and even more distressed by the lust of men. She lived in an era when no one cared what might happen to a 'commie bitch' in her mid-thirties without a husband to protect her. A widower in his fifties with seven children proposed to her once, and even worse, a male friend of her younger cousin who used to get along with her like a brother to a sister jumped over her wall one night in an attempt to rape her. Being cat-called by young male students was nothing. In the mountains, she had been a comrade as well as a revolutionary. No one had treated her as a mere woman. She bit her lips until they bled everyday, regretting that she had not died in the mountains. She could never forgive her own body, still alive and thrown as a prey to lustful men.

말로 표현할 재주가 없었던 것인지도 모른다. 이상하게 무참했고, 자꾸만 눈물이 흘렀다. 목숨을 걸었던 산에서는 나오지 않던 눈물이 살아 내려온 세상에서는 멈추지 않았다. 그는 따라 울지 않았고, 우는 그녀를 말리지도 않았다. 늦가을이었다. 소리 없는 그녀의 울음 사이로 마른 낙엽이 바람에 휩쓸렸다.

방 안에서 아무 소리도 들리지 않자 걱정스러워 문을 연 선생이 쯧쯧 혀를 찼다.

그냥 둘이 항군에 살그라. 고로코롬이라도 살아야 안 쓰겄냐.

선생의 말이 씨가 되어 둘은 사진 한 방으로 식을 대신하고 같이 살기 시작했다. 뭇 남성들의 시선에서 놓여난 것만으로도 숨을 쉴 것 같았다. 무엇보다 그와 그녀는 숱한 기억을 공유하고 있었다. 혹 누가 들을까 둘은 두꺼운 솜이불을 머리끝까지 뒤집어쓴 채 누구에게도 말할 수 없었던 지리산에서의 몇 년을 속삭이고 또 속삭였다. 만인에게 봉인된 기억이 그와 그녀만의 사랑의 밀어였다. 그 밀어 속에 딸이 태어났다. 그녀 나이 그때, 마흔둘이었다. 그 시절 마흔둘은 할머니가 되고도 남는 나이였다. 잉태도 출산도 기적이었다. 혁명에는

At that time, a man came by. He was a friend and comrade of her late husband and Pak Jong-ha. He had just returned to society after a long imprisonment.

He probably considered that it was not a good idea for two communists to get together in public, and called her to the residence of a teacher who had taught both of them. The two sat face to face in the main room with the door closed, while the old teacher was standing guard at the gate. She had thought she had countless things to talk about, but in reality, her tongue was tied. Maybe it was beyond her skills to put her countless feelings into words. Curiously, she felt only miserable, with tears flowing down from her eyes. She had never cried in the mountains where she had been ready to lay down her life, but could not stop crying in society where she was safe and alive. He neither cried with her, nor tried to stop her from crying. It was late autumn. Her silent crying was responded to by rustling fallen leaves in the wind.

Worried by silence in the room, the teacher opened the door and clicked his tongue.

"Why don't you two just live together? That's a way to live on."

When the teacher's words came true, the two took a commemorative picture instead of a wedding ceremony, and began to live together. Free from the eyes of other men, she felt she could finally

찾아와 주지 않던 기적이 그녀의 늙은 배 속에 깃든 것이었다.

딸은, 사상 말고 그녀가 찾은, 살아야 할 유일한 이유였다. 힘차게 젖을 빠는 딸을 위해 먹기 싫어도 밥을 먹었고, 딸이 끙끙 앓으며 먹는 복숭아를 사기 위해 한여름 땡볕에서 고추를 따고 말렸으며, 딸의 등록금을 마련하기 위해 허리가 굽도록 밤을 주웠다. 청춘을 산에서 보낸, 빨갱이인 그녀와 남편이 할 수 있는 일이라곤 농사밖에 없었으므로, 해본 적 없는 농사일에 몸이 녹아내렸지만 힘든 줄 몰랐다. 언제 커서 딸이 중학생이 되고, 고등학생이 되고, 대학생이 될까, 아득했던 그 세월이 이제는 외려 아득하다.

엄마!

꿈인지 생시인지 딸이 그녀를 부른다. 살짝 들춘 블라인드 너머, 긴 머리를 야무지게 양 갈래로 묶은 딸애가 보인다. 화장실에 가려는 참이었는지 딸 손에 손전등이 들려 있다. 딸이 전등을 하늘로 비춘다. 하얀 눈송이가 빛기둥 안에 갇힌다. 아이 주먹만 한 눈송이들이 빛 안에서 한 점의 흔들림도 없이 고요히 내려앉는다. 하늘과 땅 사이를 가득 메운 눈송이가 열일곱 소녀의 마음

breathe. Most of all, they shared many memories together. Over and over again, they whispered about their years in Jirisan Mountain which they had been compelled to keep to themselves, hiding under their heavy cotton-wool comforter not to be eavesdropped on by others. The memories sealed by all the others were their words of love. In lovers' whispers, a daughter was born. At that time, she was forty-two years old. That was old enough to be a grandmother in those days. Both pregnancy and delivery were miracles. Miracles had not come to her in revolution, but finally came to her old womb.

Apart from her ideology, her daughter was her only reason to live. She ate meals even if she didn't want to for the sake of her daughter sucking hard at her breast, picked and dried hot peppers under the scorching summer sun to buy peaches that her daughter was crazy about, and also picked chestnuts until she became stooped from work in order to pay her daughter's tuition. She and her husband had spent their youth as partisans in the mountains, and thus, farming was the only job they could get to make a living, to which they willingly devoted themselves, although they found the farm work strange and strenuous. It seemed to take a long time until her daughter went to middle school, and then to high school, and then to college.

을 뒤흔들어 딸은 아무도 밟지 않은 순결한 눈밭을 방방 뛰어다닌다. 딸의 움직임에 따라 갈래머리가 봄날 흰 싸리 밭의 나비처럼 나풀거린다. 캉캉, 흰 진돗개 똑순이가 딸의 뒤를 쫓아 경중경중 뛴다.

지리산에서도 그런 밤이 있었다. 천왕봉 아래였다. 이미 눈이 한길이나 쌓여 있는데 또다시 눈이 퍼부었다. 국군 일개 사단의 공격을 피해 도망 다닌 지 며칠째, 눈을 파고 눈을 요와 이불 삼아 누웠는데 또다시 폭설이 퍼부었다. 까만 밤을 배경으로 세상천지가 온통 새하얬다. 눈이 퍼부을수록 세상은 적막했다. 덮고 있는 눈도 무겁고 적막도 무거운데 마음은 자꾸만 눈송이처럼 가볍게 하늘로 날아올라 이 세상이 아닌 우주의 어떤 곳, 삶도 죽음도 뛰어넘은, 어쩌면 삶과 죽음이 시작된 어떤 곳에 닿아, 아무도 알지 못하는 생의 비의 같은 것의 정수에라도 닿은 듯한 느낌이었다. 그때, 누군가 노래를 부르기 시작했다.

태백산맥에 눈 내린다.

총을 들어라, 출정이다.

비장하거나 엄숙한 곡조가 아니었다. 그녀처럼, 눈송이처럼, 가볍게, 삶과 죽음을 뛰어넘은 자의 담담한 곡

Looking back, those past years seem to be so far away and long ago.

"Mom!"

Her daughter calls her as if in a dream. Or is it reality? Through the slightly lifted shade, she sees her daughter with her long hair meticulously braided on both sides. Presumably on the way to the outhouse, her daughter is holding a flashlight in her hand. She shines her flashlight up into the sky. White snowflakes are caught in a pole of light. Snowflakes as big as babies' fists are falling down straightforward and silent in the light. Enchanted by the great snowflakes filling the space between the sky and the earth, the seventeen-year-old girl is cheerfully running around the innocent snowfield that has not been stepped on. Along with her steps, her braided hair flutters like butterflies in a white bush clover field in spring. "Bowwow," a white Jindo dog named Smartie happily jumps around her daughter.

Once, there was a night like this in Jirisan. It was under Cheonwangbong Peak. Snow had already piled up over ten feet, and began to fall again. Chased by an ROK Army division for a few days, a group of partisans dug snow caves to sleep in, and lay in there under blankets of snow, but a heavy snowfall began again. The whole world was pure white against the pitch-dark night. The more snow

조였다. 대성골에서 대부분의 동지를 잃고 간신히 목숨
을 건져 천왕봉까지 도망친 패잔병 무리는 누구랄 것도
없이 노래를 따라 부르기 시작했다. 숨죽여 낮은 목소
리로. 가장 비참했던 시기, 그 눈 내리던 밤이, 지리산에
서의 가장 아름다운 밤이었다.

　눈송이처럼 나풀거리던 딸이 제 방으로 향한다. 오래
도록 딸의 방에는 불이 꺼지지 않는다. 그녀와 남편은
겨울의 여느 날처럼 벌레 먹어 말려놓은 밤껍질을 벗긴
다. 모여 딸의 대학 등록금이 될 밤이다. 톡톡, 밤 부스
러기가 사방으로 튄다. 톡, 딸 방의 불이 꺼진다. 달캉,
남편이 여전히 밤껍질을 벗기며 발로 문을 연다. 눈은
송이가 더 굵어진 채 여전히 쏟아지고 있다. 사락사락,
눈 내리는 소리가 산골의 적막을 더한다.

　태백산맥에 눈 내린다.

　총을 들어라, 출정이다.

　남편이 나지막이 노래를 부른다. 천왕봉 아래 폭설 퍼
붓던 그 밤처럼. 죽어도 좋았던 청춘의 시기를 거쳐, 이
제 늙은 그들은 어찌 됐든 살아야 한다. 자신들이 세상
으로 불러낸 단 한 생명을 위해. 점점 처연해지는 노랫
가락이 무거운 눈송이에 묻힌다.

poured down, the more silent the world was. The blankets of snow were heavy, and so was the absolute silence, but her heart felt like it was soaring up to the sky as lightly as snowflakes, toward a place in space outside this world, and eventually to arrive at a certain spot beyond life and death, where life and death had probably started from, and where there was the essence of life's secret meaning that no one knew. Then, someone began to sing:

Snow falls in the Taebaek Mountains.
Take your guns! It's time for war!

The tune was neither tragic nor solemn. It was as light as herself and the snowflakes, sung calmly by a human being who had transcended life and death. One by one, the remnants of the defeated Southern Army began to sing along in a low and quiet voice. They barely saved their lives and ran to Cheonwangbong Peak after having lost most of their comrades at Daeseong-gol Valley. That snowy night during her most miserable period was the most beautiful night on Jirisan.

Fluttering like a snowflake, her daughter goes back to her room. Her daughter's room is lit late into the night. As usual in winter, she and her husband peel off dried shells of worm-eaten chestnuts. The

딸이 밝힌 불빛이 오십 미터를 건너 그녀의 눈을 자극한다. 그녀가 지금 보는 단 하나의 현재다. 그녀의 달력에는 모든 수요일과 목요일에 붉은 동그라미가 그려져 있다. 딸이 근처 대학으로 출강하는 날이다. 딸이 없는 날은 수요일과 목요일, 그녀의 세상은 그날을 중심으로 돌아간다. 그마저도 간혹 헷갈리지만 그녀의 시야에 딸의 차가 보이지 않으면 그날은 수요일이거나 목요일이다. 딸의 차가 보이는 날은 무슨 요일이든 상관이 없다. 딸이 늘 제 집에 있을 것이므로. 그런 날은 달력을 볼 일도 없다. 세상은 딸을 중심으로 돌고, 그녀의 세상은 멈춘 지 오래다.

수요일과 목요일, 그녀는 일곱 시 즈음이면 창가에 붙어 앉아 블라인드를 살짝 들춘 채 하염없이 밖을 내다본다. 딸이 옆방에서 돌아눕는 기척도 알아채던 그녀의 귀는 이제 바로 집 옆으로 지나는 딸의 차 소리도 듣지 못한다. 눈으로 보는 것 외엔 길이 없어 그녀는 깜깜한 어둠을 응시한 채 상향등 불빛이 달려오기를, 딸 집의 불이 켜지기를 학수고대할 뿐이다. 딸의 차는 대개 일곱 시에서 일곱 시 십 분이면 정확하게 늘 서던 그 자리에 선다. 간혹 더 늦어질 때도 있다. 그런 날, 그녀의 심

chestnuts will help her pay her daughter's college tuition. "Click click," chestnut crumbs are scattered in all directions. "Click," the light is turned off in her daughter's room. "Thrump," her husband opens the door with his foot while peeling off chestnut shells with his hands. Even bigger snowflakes are still pouring down. "Crisp," the sound of snow falling deepens the silence in the mountain village.

Snow falls in the Taebaek Mountains.
Take your guns! It's time for war!

Her husband sings the song in a low voice, like he did on the night of heavy snowfall under Cheonwangbong Peak. They lived their youth for a cause worth dying for, and now, the old couple have to survive, like it or not, for a life they have brought to the earth. His saddening voice is buried under heavy snowflakes.

Her eyes are irritated by the light from her daughter's house at a fifty-meter distance. It is the only present that she sees now. On her calendar, every Wednesday and Thursday are checked in red. These are the days when her daughter gives lectures at a nearby university. Her daughter is absent on Wednesdays and Thursdays, and her world is centered on these days. If her daughter's car is out of her sight, it is either Wednesday or

장은 그 옛날, 지리산에서 전투를 하던 때처럼 펄떡거린다. 언젠가 딸이 예고도 없이 두 시간이나 늦은 적이 있다. 시계를 탁자 위에 놓아두고 그녀는 자꾸 시계를 봤다. 영겁 같은 시간이 흐른 듯한데 고작 분침이 한 칸 움직였을 뿐이었다. 숨이 꼴깍 넘어갈 것 같다는 말을, 그녀는 오랜만에 실감했다. 그 시간 동안 딸은 강사 자리를 유지하기 위해 잘 보여야 하는 전임교수들과 저녁을 먹었다. 딸의 일상이 사소하게 흔들리면 그녀의 삶에서는 우주가 흔들린다. 전 남편의 죽음 앞에서도 초연했던 그녀다. 사상을 잃은 뒤로 딸이 그녀의 사상이 되었고, 딸이라는 사상 앞에서는 잠시도 초연할 수 없다. 사상이 위대한 것인지, 혈육이 위대한 것인지 그녀는 알지 못한다.

딸에 대한 사소한 걱정들이 오히려 딸의 발목을 잡는 짓임을 모르지 않는다. 딸의 말마따나 그녀 걱정의 구십구 퍼센트는 죄 쓸데없는 걱정이었다. 그런데도 딸만 생각하면 쓸데없는 걱정이 창조적으로 떠오른다. 딸은 평생 그녀의 걱정거리였다. 좋은 대학을 갈까, 좋은 직장을 구할까, 착한 남자를 만날까, 둘이 잘 살까, 걱정이 무색하게 딸은 잘 살았고, 잘 살고 있다. 정확하지 않고

Thursday, although even this is confusing sometimes. If the car is in sight, it doesn't matter what day it is, since her daughter must be home all day long. She doesn't need to look at the calender on such days. The world rotates on the axis of her daughter; her world stopped long ago.

On Wednesdays and Thursdays, she sits close by the window at seven o'clock in the evening, looking out the window absentmindedly with the shade slightly open. Her ears used to notice the sound of her daughter turning over in bed in the next room, but now cannot hear the sound of her daughter's car passing right by her house. Since seeing is the only way for her, she is looking at pitch darkness, eagerly waiting for her daughter's car to arrive home with its lights on high beam, and for her daughter's house to be lit. Usually, her daughter parks the car in the same spot punctually between 7:00 and 7:10 p.m. Sometimes her daughter comes back later than that. On such days, her heart palpitates fast just like it did at the battlefields of Jirisan long ago. One day, her daughter came home two hours late without notice. She put her clock on the table and watched it over and over. It seemed like a lifetime, but the long hand of the clock moved only a minute's space. She felt like choking to death after a long time. That night, her daughter was having dinner with faculty members whom she needed to

꼼꼼하지 못한 게 어려서부터 걱정이었는데, 꼼꼼하지 못한 것은 까다롭지 않은 것, 정확하지 않은 것은 여유로운 것이었는지, 두루두루 잘 어울리고 사람 덕 보며, 이날 입때껏 문제 하나 일으키지 않았다. 딸의 유일한 걱정거리는 제 남편도 아니요 자식도 아니요, 바로 그녀다. 특별히 무엇이 문제는 아니다. 늙어도 죽지 않는 어미라는 존재 자체가 골칫덩이다.

그녀는 자신이 짐이 되는 상황을 꿈에도 생각해보지 않았다. 산에서 죽을 고생을 한 탓에 온갖 병을 끼고 살아, 어린 딸을 두고 일찍 죽을 것만이 걱정이었다. 초등학교에 입학하는 거라도 보고 죽었으면, 교복 입는 것이나 보고 죽었으면, 했다. 대학에 입학했을 때는 더 이상 바랄 것이 없었다. 딸이 결혼했을 때는 덤 같은 행복을 누렸고, 손자가 태어났을 때는 내가 이렇게 행복해도 되나, 이렇게 오래 살아도 되나 싶었다. 그 손자가 자라 벌써 대학생이 되었다. 산에서 죽었어야 할 사람이 이렇게나 오래 살아남았다.

남편이 살아있을 때까지만 해도 그녀는 짐 덩이가 아니었다. 남편을 거두고 살림을 사는 주부였다. 그때는 해마다 장을 담아 딸에게 보내고, 철철이 딸과 사위가

appeal to in order to keep her position as a lecturer. If the daily life of her daughter falters a little, the whole universe falters in her life. She used to remain undisturbed, even by the death of her first husband. After she lost her ideology, her daughter alone became her new ideology, and from this new ideology, she cannot remain aloof even for a minute. She does not know whether ideology is great, or flesh and blood is great.

She is not unaware that her trivial worries as a parent will shackle her daughter instead. As her daughter says, ninety-nine percent of her worries are absolutely useless. Still, whenever she thinks about her daughter, she spontaneously creates useless worries. Her daughter has been her concern all her life. Would she go to a good college? Would she get a good job? Would she find a good man? Would she have a good marriage? Her daughter has lived well, and is living well, banishing all her worries. She was worried that her daughter was neither perfectionistic nor meticulous enough as a child, but probably her lack of meticulousness implied a lack of pickiness, and her lack of perfectionism implied a lack of nervousness. To this very day, her daughter has never made any trouble, getting along with a lot of friends and benefitting from their friendship. Her daughter's only worry is neither her husband nor her child; it is her. There is no particular problem. The

좋아하는 온갖 나물을 캐고 다듬고 씻고 삶아 라면 박
스에 가득 담아 보냈다. 지팡이 짚은 채 산으로 들로 다
니며 애들 좋아하는 나물 캐는 게 그 무렵의 유일한 낙
이었다. 그때는 그러니까 자식을 위해 뭐라도 해주는
진짜 어미였던 것이다. 어미이자 사회인이기도 했다.
남편이 치매에 걸리기 전까지는 밤마다 아홉시 뉴스를
봤고, 정세를 논했으며, 덕분에 세상 돌아가는 것도 어
느 정도는 알고 있었다.

　남편이 치매 진단을 받았을 때 이제 하늘이 그만 죽
으라는구나 싶었다. 그녀도 남편도 목숨에 별 미련은
없었다. 다만 딸에게 짐이 되는, 오래 앓는 병만은 피했
으면 했다. 치매는 그중 으뜸이었다. 남편보다 두어 해
먼저 친정 여동생이 치매에 걸렸다. 저 살기 바빴던 자
식들은 가차 없이 요양원으로 보내버렸다. 소식만 듣고
오래 본 적 없는 동생을, 남편 치매 진단받고 마지막으
로 보러 갔다. 동생은 무릎을 세우고 앉아 가랑이 사이
에 고개를 처박고 있었다. 이름을 불러도 고개조차 들
지 않았다. 가만 보니 오른손이 빠른 속도로 일정하게
움직이고 있었다.

　아유, 또 이러시네. 내가 미쳐, 정말!

very existence of an elderly mother who would not die of old age is a nuisance.

Never did she dream that she would become a burden to her daughter. She was only worried that she might die early while her daughter was a child, since she was suffering from various diseases resulting from extreme hardships she had gone through in the mountains. She only wished that she could live long enough to see her daughter enter elementary school, and then, to see her daughter in high school uniform. There was nothing more she could wish for when her daughter entered college. The marriage of her daughter was just more icing on the cake for her, and the birth of her grandson made her wonder if it was all right for her to be so happy and to live so long. Her grandson has already grown up to be a college student. She should have died in the mountains, but has survived for such a long time.

She was not a burden while her husband was still alive. She was a housewife taking care of her husband. Back then, she used to send her daughter homemade soy sauce and soybean paste every year. For her daughter and son-in-law, she would gather, wash, trim and boil their favorite wild greens so that she could send her daughter ramen boxes full of seasoned vegetables each and every season. In those days, her only delight was to

뒤따라온 요양사가 호들갑스럽게 동생에게 달려들었다. 동생의 팔을 붙잡아 상체를 들어 올리자 흰 시트 위에 선혈이 낭자했다. 아랫도리는 홀딱 벗은 채였다. 동생은 온 힘을 다해 팔과 다리를 버둥거렸다. 동생의 은밀한 부위가 환한 햇빛 아래 낯선 물건인 양 생경하게 드러났다. 요양사가 버튼을 누르자 급히 달려온 남자 둘이 발버둥치는 동생의 사지를 침대 네 귀퉁이에 묶었다.

그녀와 동생은 일곱 살 터울이었다. 동생이 첫 울음을 터뜨리기도 전에 어머니의 가랑이 사이에서 분수처럼 피가 솟구쳤다. 한쪽 벽이 온통 붉게 물들었다. 맥을 놓기 직전 어머니가 그녀의 팔을 붙잡았다. 무어라 말을 했으나 겁에 질린 그녀는 알아듣지 못했다. 아니, 듣지는 못했어도 알았다. 이제 막 떨궈놓은 핏덩이를 부탁한다는 말이었을 것이다. 자신의 모든 에너지를 전하려는 것인지 죽어가는 어머니의 아귀힘이 점점 강해졌다. 죽은 뒤에도 어머니의 손은 그녀의 가는 팔목을 그러쥐고 있었다. 아버지가 어머니의 손가락을 일일이 떼어냈다. 어찌나 억세게 쥐고 있었는지 죽은 어머니의 손가락에서 툭 툭, 뼈 부러지는 소리가 났다. 오래도록 그녀는 죽은 어머니가 자신의 팔에 매달려 있는 느낌이었

wander around mountains and fields with the aid of a cane to gather their favorite wild greens. At that time, then, she was a real mother doing something for her daughter. She was also a member of society. Before her husband went senile, she had watched the news on television every night, discussing political affairs, knowledgeable, to an extent, about the ways the world worked.

When her husband was diagnosed with Alzheimer's disease, she thought that her time had come. Both she and her husband had no regrets about life. Yet, they wished that they could avoid terminal diseases that would last long and burden their daughter. Alzheimer's was on the top of the list. Her younger sister had gone senile two or three years before her husband did. Her nephews and nieces, who were busy feeding themselves, put their mother in a nursing home without mercy. After her husband's diagnosis, she went to see her sister for the last time, whom she had heard from but not seen for a long while. Her sister was sitting with her knees up, ducking her head between her legs. She didn't even raise her head when she called her name. She looked at her sister closely to find that her right hand was moving rapidly at a steady pace.

"Gosh! There you go again. You're driving me crazy!"

다. 어머니가 팔을 꽉 움켜쥐는 것 같아 어머니요? 어머니 왔소? 자다 벌떡 일어난 적도 부지기수였다. 열일곱 살 초봄, 시집갈 날을 받아놓고 그녀는 어머니 묘를 찾았다. 어머니 간 뒤로 하루에도 서너 차례씩 찾던 곳이었다. 어머니 좋아하던 진달래를 한 아름 꺾어 묘 앞에 놓고 평소처럼 퍼질러 앉았는데 웬일인지 등골이 서늘했다. 온몸의 털이 바싹 곤두섰다.

가그라. 다시는 오지 말그라.

어머니의 호통소리가 차가운 뱀처럼 온몸을 휘감았다. 살아생전 한 번도 그녀를 나무라본 적 없는 어머니였다. 무섬증에 그녀는 뒤도 안 돌아보고 한 걸음에 산을 내려왔다. 그 뒤로 팔에 매달려 있던 어머니가 사라졌다. 무서워서 어머니 무덤에도 다시 가지 못했다.

죽은 어머니 대신 그녀가 동생의 어머니였다. 갓난쟁이를 들쳐 업은 채 젖동냥을 다니고, 쌀뜨물로 미음을 끓여 먹였다. 기저귀 가는 것도 빠는 것도 삶는 것도 일곱 살 그녀 몫이었다. 기저귀를 갈 때만 잠깐 바람을 쐬는 동생의 그곳은 입을 꾹 다문 조개처럼 야무지고 희고 어여뻤다. 치자 꽃처럼 보얀 사타구니며 궁둥이가 아직도 눈에 선했다. 그러나 아이 넷을 출산한 동생의

The caretaker who had followed her flung herself on her sister dramatically, grabbing her sister's arms to raise her upper body. The white sheet was saturated with fresh blood. The lower part of her sister's body was stark naked. Her sister was struggling and swinging her limbs wildly. Her sister's sex was revealed in the raw under bright sunlight, like something weird. As soon as the caretaker pushed a button, two men rushed to the scene to tie her struggling sister's limbs to the four corners of the bed.

Her sister was seven years younger than her. Even before her sister cried her first cry, blood spurted like a fountain from between her mother's legs. The wall on one side turned red with splattered blood. Her mother grabbed her arm immediately before her death. Her mother murmured some words, but she was too frightened to grasp them. Yet, she knew, although she did not hear her clearly, that her mother must have asked her to take care of the newborn baby just delivered. The grip of her dying mother became stronger and stronger, as if trying to give all her energy to her offspring. Even after death, the hands of her deceased mother were still grabbing her slender wrist. Her father tore her mother's fingers from her wrist one by one. "Tap tap," the grip was so strong that she could hear the sound of bones breaking in the fingers of her

그곳은 헤지고 닳아 생전 삶아본 적 없는 걸레처럼 거무스름했다. 그녀는 참을 수 없는 모욕을 당한 느낌이었다. 이불 덮어줄 생각도 않고 다 쓴 물건인 양 마구잡이로 다루는 요양사 때문이 아니었다. 태어나자마자 어미 잃고 북풍한설에 갈 데 없는 한 마리 노루처럼 바들바들 떨며 한평생을 견뎌온 사람에게 최소한 이런 마지막이 기다리고 있어서는 안 되는 것이었다. 그러나 누가 동생에게 이런 마지막을 준비한 것인지 알 수 있을리 만무했다. 그러니 이 모욕감은 준 자가 없는 것, 견딜밖에 도리가 없었다. 신으로부터, 혹은 삶으로부터 모욕당한 당사자가 모욕조차 이미 잊었다는 게 축복이라면 축복이었다.

그녀가 그런 생각을 하는 동안에도 사지 묶인 동생은 궁둥이를 쳐들고 허리를 비틀며 요분질 치는 흉내를 내고 있었다. 입에서는 연신 가쁜 숨소리가 새어 나왔다. 새어 나왔다는 건 정확하지 않다. 부끄러움도 모두 잊은 동생은 절정의 탄성을 세상 사람 모두 들으라는 듯 고래고래 외쳤다. 손으로 얼마나 야무지게 후빈 것인지 하늘로 쳐든 동생의 그곳에서는 여전히 붉은 피가 흐르고 있었다.

deceased mother. For a long period of time, she felt like her deceased mother was clinging to her arm. On countless nights, she leaped out of bed, saying, "Mother? Is it you?" She felt like her mother was grabbing her arm hard. At the age of seventeen when her wedding day was set, she visited her mother's grave in early spring. She had been visiting the grave several times a day after her mother's death. She picked a bunch of azaleas which had been her mother's favorite, offered them to the grave, and sat down carelessly as usual. All of a sudden, without knowing why, she got chills down her spine. Her hair bristled all over her body at once.

"Go away! Don't ever come here again!"

The thundering voice of her mother twined around her entire body like a cold snake. Her mother had never scolded her in life. Frightened and terrified, she hurried down the mountain without looking back and without a break. Afterwards, her mother, clinging to her arm, disappeared. She was so terrified that she never visited her mother's grave again.

On behalf of her deceased mother, she became a mother to her sister. Carrying her infant sister on her back, she solicited breast milk from other mothers, and fed the baby with thin rice gruel made from the starchy water when washing rice.

아유, 정말. 기저귀를 채워도 소용없고 어쩌면 좋아. 정조대라도 채워야 할까 봐요.

그녀는 바닥에 흘러내린 이불을 주워 동생에게 덮었다. 그러나 동생의 발버둥에 이내 또다시 흘러내렸다.

놀라셨죠? 첨이라 놀라셨을 거예요. 근데 이런 분들 많아요. 그래도 이분은 양반이에요. 하루 종일 자위만 하는 할머니도 있어요. 할아버지들이야 뭐……. 꼴에 남자라고 덮치기도 해요. 할머니들은 그래도 덮치지는 않으니까. 자기들 상처가 나서 그렇지.

요양사는 능숙한 솜씨로 한쪽 다리의 매듭을 풀고 속옷과 바지를 꿴 뒤, 다른 다리도 마저 꿰었다. 그리고 다시 침대에 묶었다.

동생은 그녀가 시집간 뒤 어미 잃은 강아지처럼 기가 죽었다. 재취 얻은 아버지는 고작 열다섯 먹은 동생을 윗동네 땅꾼에게 시집보냈다. 제부는 뱀을 잡고 동생은 산나물을 캐 네 아이를 먹여 살렸다. 먹는 날보다 굶는 날이 더 많았지만 자식들 모두 죽지 않고 살아남았다. 뱀 먹어 그런지 힘 하나는 좋았던 제부는 동생이 스물일곱 되던 해 뱀에 물려 세상을 떠났다. 그날 이후 어린 새끼들 살리느라 동생은 남자에게 눈길 한 번 줄 수 없

As a seven-year-old girl, she changed, washed and boiled her sister's diapers. When changing diapers, she saw her sister's sex exposed briefly, fair and lovely, as firm as a tightly closed clam. The baby's milky buttocks and crotch, as white as gardenia flowers, were still vivid before her eyes. Her sister delivered four children, and her sex came to look dark and worn out, like a dirty rag that has never been washed. It seemed an unbearable insult to her sister. It was not because of the caretaker who didn't bother to cover her sister with a blanket, and carelessly treated her like a used up thing. This should not, at least, be the end for a person who had lost her mother at birth, and had lived her whole life shivering like a roe deer stranded with nowhere to go in windy and snowy winter. Yet, there was no way to figure out who had prepared this ending for her sister. This insult was given by no one, and therefore, all she could do was to endure it. The only blessing was that the one insulted by God, or by life, had already forgotten the insult.

While she was thinking these thoughts, her tied up sister was mimicking sexual intercourse, lifting her pelvis and twisting her waist. Her sister was incessantly gasping for breath. Gasping was not an accurate way to put it. Totally unashamed, her sister was shouting at the top of her lungs, as if she

는 세월을 살았다. 사느라 바빠 돌아보지 못했던 성욕이 기억을 잃자 기어이 나 여기 있노라, 제 존재를 드러낸 것일까. 죽어가는 몸뚱어리에서 꾸역꾸역 기어 나와 제 존재를 증명하려는 욕망이라는 것이 생명을 이 세상으로 보냈을 터, 따져보면 욕망이 곧 생명이었다. 제 몸속에도 도사리고 있을 생명인지 욕망인지 그 뭔가가, 그녀는 도무지 수그러들 줄 모르는 한여름의 뙤약볕처럼 지긋지긋했다. 어머니였던 언니가 오는지 가는지도 모르고 동생은 마지막 욕망의 축제에 달떠 있었다.

동생에게 다녀온 뒤 그녀는 빠릿빠릿해졌다. 남편까지 그 꼴로 만들 수는 없었다. 다행히 남편은 동생과 증상이 달랐다. 남편이 세상에서 제일 좋아하는 건 술, 담배, 그리고 사람이었다. 매일 소주 세 병을 마셨지만 한 자리에서 오래 마시는 법이 없어 평생 취한 모습을 보이지는 않았다. 치매가 걸린 뒤 남편은 방금 술 마신 것을, 방금 담배 피운 것을 잊어버렸다. 그녀는 시시때때로 남편의 옷을 뒤져 악착같이 술 마실 돈을 뺏고 담배를 뺏었다. 치매 걸린 남편은 전과 달리 버럭버럭 잘도 성질을 부렸다. 치매 수발 삼 년에 그녀는 고혈압, 고지혈증, 골다공증, 당뇨를 얻었다. 환갑 때부터 미운 친구

had wanted the whole world to hear her orgasmic exclamation. Her sister poked herself there with her finger so fiercely that blood was still running from that place lifted up in the air.

"Gosh! Diapers are useless. What should I do? Maybe she needs a chastity belt."

The caretaker picked up her sister's blanket from the floor and put it over her. It slipped down again, however, in no time due to her sister's struggle.

"Are you surprised? No wonder you're surprised because this is your first time. By the way, many patients are like her. She is the best of a bad bunch. Another old lady is playing with herself all day long. Not to mention old men. . . Some of them try to rape women at that age. They are so pathetic. Elderly women don't attack others at least. They just hurt themselves."

The caretaker skillfully untied one of her sister's legs and put it in one opening of panties and trousers, and untied the other leg and put it in the other. The caretaker then tied her sister's legs back to the corners of the bed.

After she had married and left home, her sister grew dispirited like a motherless puppy. Her father got a second wife, and married off her sister, who was only fifteen years old, to a snake hunter in the neighboring village. Her sister's husband hunted snakes, while her sister gathered wild greens to

처럼 함께 해온 척추협착증은 더 심해져 집안에서도 지팡이 없이는 서너 발도 뗄 수 없을 정도였다. 그 삼 년간 남편과 지독히도 싸웠다.

지발 존 일에 술 담배 쫌 끊으씨요. 먼 놈의 핵멩가가 술 담배 한나를 못 끊는다요! 완전히 멍충이가 되불믄 워쩔라고 그요? 빨갱이 딸이라고 대학교수도 못 됐는디, 가난배끼 물레준 것이 없음서 인자 짐뎅이꺼정 될라 그요?

하루에도 수십 번씩 그녀는 고함을 질렀다. 멍청하게 허공만 응시하던 남편은 어쩌다 한 번씩 골을 냈다.

나가 멋땀시 짐뎅이가 돼! 그럴라면 칵 쎗바닥을 깨물고 죽어불랑게 걱정 붙들어 매소.

큰소리치던 남편이 바지에 똥을 지리고 들어왔을 때 그녀는 눈앞이 캄캄했다. 움직이는 종합병원이나 다름없는 여든 넘은 그녀에게는 겨울 바지 빠는 것조차 힘에 부쳤다. 하루에도 서너 번씩 똥을 지리면 남편보다 그녀가 먼저 죽을 것 같았고, 그러면 치매 걸린 제 아버지 모른 척할 리 없는 딸까지 죽어 나갈 터였다. 이 노릇을 어쩌나, 그녀는 차가운 화장실 타일 바닥에 주저앉아 똥 묻은 바지를 빨며 온갖 생각을 다 했다. 그래, 쥐

raise their four children. Starving days outnumbered days of eating, but all of the children managed to survive. Her sister's husband was physically powerful probably because he had eaten lots of snakes, but died from a snake bite when her sister was twenty-seven years old. Afterwards, she was too busy raising young children to flirt with men all her life. She wondered if her sister's sexual drive, long forgotten while living from hand to mouth, finally revealed itself once her sister lost memory. It had been there all along. The thing called desire, which was creeping out of the dying body to prove its existence persistently, brought life to this world, and therefore, desire was life itself by any measure. She was disgusted with the thing, whether life or desire, which must be lurking also in her body, like the scorching midsummer sun that would never die down. Her sister was full of excitement at the last feast of desire, without recognizing the presence of her elder sister who had also been her mother.

After the visit to her sister, she took a hold of herself. She would not let her husband get worse like her sister. Luckily, her husband's symptoms were different from those of her sister. Her husband's favorite things were alcohol, cigarettes and people. He drank three bottles of soju everyday, but did not drink much in one place, and thus, was never seen drunk in public. With

약이든 농약이든, 한날한시에 같이 죽자. 산에서 진작 죽어야 했을 사람들, 죽어도 여한이 없다. 그게 그녀의 결론이었다.

어깨를 짓누르는 낡은 코트를 입고 그녀는 오랜만에 길을 나섰다. 지리산에서 매서운 바람이 불어 그녀의 길을 막았다. 한 걸음 걷고 한 걸음 밀리고 도무지 걸음이 나아가질 않았다. 지리산에서는 때로 인간의 접근을 허용하지 않으려는 산신령의 불호령인 듯 무시무시한 바람이 불었다. 영하 사십 도를 훌쩍 넘는 한겨울에도 누더기에 짚신 차림으로 그녀와 동지들은 거침없이 그 바람을 뚫고 지리산을 누볐다. 지금 그녀의 앞길을 막는 바람 따위는 유도 아니었다. 그런데도 여든 넘은 그녀는 옛날과 비교하면 봄밤 훈풍 같은 바람을 뚫고 나가지 못했다. 그녀는 지팡이에 의지한 채 버티고 서서 지리산을 바라보았다. 지리산에서 일어나 그녀에게 다가온 바람이 귓가에 무어라 속삭였다.

우리 맹꺼정 다 얹어 줬응게 원 없이 살다 오시게.

더 살고 싶은 원 따위, 없었다. 차라리 죽는 게 원이었다. 그러나 저 편하자고 하나뿐인 딸의 가슴에 평생 지워지지 않을 한을 남길 수는 없는 노릇이었다. 산에서

Alzheimer's disease, however, he forgot the fact that he had just had a drink or a smoke. She rummaged through his clothes every now and then, and ruthlessly took his cigarettes and drinking money. Unlike before, her senile husband lost his temper frequently and frantically. During the three years she looked after him, she developed high blood pressure, hyperlipidemia, osteoporosis and diabetes. Spinal stenosis, which had been with her like a naughty friend since the age of sixty, became so bad that she could not walk a few steps without a cane even within doors. During those three years, she and her husband fought like cats and dogs.

"Please stop drinking and smoking for God's sake. What kind of revolutionary can't quit drinking and smoking? What are you going to do if you become a complete idiot? Your daughter couldn't become a professor because she was a commie's daughter. All you left her was poverty, and now, do you want to be a burden, too?"

She yelled at him dozens of times a day. Her husband usually stared into the air stupidly, and threw a tantrum once in a while.

"Why would I become a burden? I'd rather bite my tongue and die, so never mind."

Having been so boastful and proud, her husband came home in pooped pants one day, which completely panicked her. Over the age of eighty,

도, 밖에서도, 죽는 것 하나 마음대로 되지 않았다.

절대로 짐 덩이가 되지 않겠다던 남편은 난생처음 똥을 지린 일주일 뒤, 자전거를 타고 가다 전봇대를 들이받았다. 병원까지 멀쩡하게 걸어간 남편은 세 시간 뒤 의식을 잃었고, 그 뒤로 다시는 깨어나지 않았다. 병원 침상에서 벌떡 일어나 비척비척 걸으며, 어이, 집에 가세, 라고 한 것이 남편의 마지막 말이었다. 출혈 때문에 부은 뇌가 뇌간을 누르기까지, 그래서 숨이 끊어지기까지, 의사는 일주일에서 보름 정도 걸릴 거라 했다. 밤새 순천으로 달려온 딸이 간병을 하고 그녀가 옷가지며 이불을 챙기러 사위 차로 집에 다니러 간 새, 남편은 서둘러 세상을 떴다. 짐 덩이가 되지 않겠다더니 잠시 고생할 시간조차 주지 않은 것이다. 이리 갈 것을, 그것도 모르고 딸 생각만 하느라 악착같이 술 담배 못하게 한 것이 미안해서, 쥐약 살 생각한 것이 미안해서, 다시 깨어나지 못할 거라는 의사 말에 차라리 다행이라 안도한 것이 미안해서, 그녀는 장례식장에서 섧게 울었다. 첫 남편 갈 때는 한 방울도 주지 않은 눈물이었다.

금방 따라갈라요. 먼저 가서 자리 잡고 있으씨요이.

이번에도 그녀는 금방 따라가지 못했다. 얼마 뒤, 딸

she was a so-called 'walking general hospital' suffering from a variety of health issues, and even washing heavy winter pants was too much work for her. She was likely to die before her husband if he continued to poop in his pants several times a day, and then, her daughter, who could not turn a blind eye to her senile father, would almost die as well. What should she do? While she was sitting on the cold tile floor of the bathroom and washing his dirty pants, all kinds of thoughts flashed through her mind. Yes, either by rat poison or by pesticide, they should die together on the same day and time. They should have died in the mountains long ago, so they could die without regrets. That was her conclusion.

For the first time in years, she hit the road again in her old coat too heavy for her shoulders. A bitter wind blowing from Jirisan Mountain blocked the way. Taking one step forward and one step backward, she could not go forward at all. In the mountains, ghastly winds used to blow from time to time, as if the mountain god had given a strict command not to allow human approach. Even when the temperature had fallen to forty degrees below zero in midwinter, she and her comrades in rags and straw shoes had crisscrossed the mountain against the harsh wind without hesitation. The wind she was facing was nothing compared to

이 계약직 교수를 때려치우고 저 혼자 윗집을 얻어 내려왔던 것이다. 한사코 마다해도 딸 역시 남편 고집을 닮아 쇠귀에 경 읽기였다. 딸의 경력을 망친 듯해 마음이 편치 않았지만 내심 좋았다. 곧 남편을 따라갈 테니 몇 달 정도는 매일 딸의 얼굴을 보는 호사쯤 누려도 괜찮지 않을까 싶기도 했다. 웬걸, 남편이 죽으면서 자기가 만든 병까지 죄 가져간 모양인지 혈압도 고지혈증도 골다공증도 당뇨도 깨끗이 사라졌다. 딸이 하루가 멀다고 읍내 병원에 데리고 다닌 덕도 있을 것이고, 고기며 생선이며, 칼로리 계산해서 대령하는 삼시 세끼 덕도 있긴 했을 것이다. 고질병인 척추협착증이야 여전하지만 그 또한 딸의 우격다짐으로 받은 신경 마비 시술 덕분에 그럭저럭 참을 만하다. 스물 넘어 이렇게 몸이 개운한 적은 처음이다. 딸이 내려온 뒤로 그 흔한 감기 한번 걸린 적이 없다. 몇 달만 누릴 작정이었던 호사가 벌써 십삼 년째다.

긍게, 우리 맹꺼정 원 없이 살다 오라고 안 그랬소. 실컨 사씨요. 죽을 때꺼정 사씨요.

코앞의 지리산에서는 시도 때도 없이 바람이 일어 칡꽃이며 밤꽃이며 온갖 내음을 실어나르고, 거기 기대

it. Yet, over the age of eighty, she could not move forward against the wind that was merely a warm spring breeze compared to what it had been before. Leaning on her cane, she stood still and looked at Jirisan. The wind rising from the mountain came to her and whispered something in her ear: "We gave you our share of life, so please live as long as you wish before you come back to us!"

The wish to live on was not hers. She wished, rather, that she would die. Death would be convenient for her, but she could not make her daughter, her only flesh and blood, live in regret that would last for the rest of her daughter's life. Either in or out of the mountains, dying was beyond her control.

While her husband had assured her that he would never be a burden, the bicycle he was riding hit an electric pole one week after the day he had pooped in his pants for the first time. He walked to a hospital unscathed, but lost consciousness three hours later never to wake up again. In hospital, he sprang out of bed and staggered, saying, "Hey, let's go home!," which were his last words. The doctor said that it would take one or two weeks for his injured brain, swollen from internal bleeding, to put pressure on his brain stem and eventually to kill him. That night, her daughter drove all through the night to Suncheon and nursed him, while her son-in-law gave her a ride home for clothes and

살고 죽은 모든 것들의 눈물이며 웃음 같은 것들을 그녀의 눈앞에 펼쳐 놓는다.

이것 잠 묵어보써요.

보급투쟁 나갔던 박종하가 그녀에게 고깃덩이를 내민다. 아무 의심 없이 그녀는 그것을 받아먹는다. 아무리 씹어도 씹어지질 않는다. 하얗게 박종하가 배를 잡고 웃는다. 알고 보니 박종하가 준 것은 소의 그것이다. 박종하는 틈만 나면 그녀를 놀린다.

이 여성이 말이여. 참말로 위대한 여성이여. 소 고것 꺼정 묵었당게.

박종하의 웃음소리가 보청기도 떼어놓은 그녀의 귓가에 왕왕거린다. 죽음을 각오한 동지들이, 오전 전투에서 동지를 아홉이나 잃은 동지들이, 자신들의 무덤이 될 곳에서 호탕하게 웃음을 터뜨린다. 이상도 하지. 언젠가부터 죽은 자들의 얼굴이 환하게 밝아온다. 오히려 산 자들의 얼굴은 안개 속인 듯 부옇다. 오늘 낮에 본 딸애 친구의 얼굴은 지금 또 봐도 모를 것이다. 딸 친구가 그녀 먹으라고 과자를 다섯 박스나 사 왔다. 대만 여행 가서 사온 파인애플 케이크라고 했다. 태어나서 먹은 것 중에 제일 맛났다. 맛을 잃은 지 오래, 오랜만에 입이

blankets, and in the meantime, her husband passed away in haste. Having assured her that he would not be a burden, he gave her no time to suffer. She sobbed her heart out at his funeral because she was sorry for having kept him from drinking and smoking cold-bloodedly for the sake of her daughter without knowing that he would die like this. She was sorry for having thought of buying rat poison, and she was sorry for having felt relieved by the doctor's statement that he would never regain his consciousness, considering it better for him. She had not shed a single teardrop for the death of her first husband.

"I will follow you soon. Go first and wait for me!"

But she failed to follow him soon. After a while, her daughter quit her job as an adjunct professor, and moved next door to her alone. She vehemently protested the idea, but her daughter, being as stubborn as her husband, turned a deaf ear to her. She felt uneasy because it might ruin her daughter's career, but was happy at heart. She was bound to follow her husband soon, so it seemed reasonable to enjoy the brief luxury of seeing her daughter everyday for a few months. But whoops! Her dead husband must have taken away all of the diseases that he had caused. Her high blood pressure, hyper-lipidemia, osteoporosis and diabetes are all gone now. Her daughter takes her to a clinic in town

달콤해 하나를 더 먹었다. 아흔아홉에 제일 맛있는 걸 만나다니, 이러려고 이날까지 살았나 싶다.

딸이 내려온 뒤 평생 못 먹어본 오만 걸 다 먹었다. 송이니 능이니, 전복이니 굴이니, 대합이니 백합이니, 동파육이니 유산슬이니, 가기 전에 원 없이 먹이려는 딸 맘을 모르는 바는 아니나 이미 맛을 잃은 그녀 입에는 어떤 것도 된장국만 못했다. 다만 눈은 호강이었다. 딸이 차려준 밥상을 볼 때마다 그녀는 죽은 남편이 생각났다. 산에서 열흘 굶은 남편은 보급투쟁을 나가던 길에 정신을 잃고 쓰러졌다. 동지들이 돌아오는 길, 의식 잃은 그에게 동지 목숨 몇과 바꾼 날달걀 하나를 깨 입에 넣어주었다. 달걀이 위에 닿는 순간 그는 눈을 떴다. 그 뒤로 밥은 그에게 자동차 움직이는 기름이었다.

얼른 지름 묵세.

그게 상 차리라는 말이었다. 산에서 죽은 동지들이나 남편에게 밥은 맛을 따지기 전에 몸을 움직이는 연료였다. 비싼 돈 들여 맛있는 것 사 먹는 재미를 그들도 그녀도 알지 못했다. 그런 세월을 살았다. 손 큰 딸은 뭐든 넉넉하게 해서 남은 것은 아까운 줄 모르고 다 버렸다. 그게 아까워 몰래 숨겨두고 꾸역꾸역 먹으면 딸은 벽력

almost everyday, and serves her three meals made of beef and fish, with calories counted for her. She still has chronic spinal stenosis, but it is somewhat bearable due to the neurosurgery treatment urged by her daughter. She has never felt more refreshed in her adult life. Since her daughter moved next door to her, she has not even had a common cold. She wanted to enjoy this luxury only for a few months, but it turned out to last for thirteen years.

"So, we told you that we had given you our share of life. Please live as long as you wish! Live as long as you breathe!"

From Jirisan standing right in front of her house, the wind blows in and out of season, bringing the scents of kudzu flowers and chestnut blossoms, and showing her the tears and laughter of all beings whose life and death depended on the mountain.

"Have a bite of this!"

Pak Jong-ha gives her a piece of meat that he has brought from a supply struggle.[3] She puts it in her mouth without any doubt. No matter how long she tries to chew, it won't be chewed. Pak shakes with laughter like an innocent child. The thing he gave her turns out to be the private parts of a bull. He jokes with her at every opportunity.

"This lady is indeed a great woman. She even ate

3) Supply struggle refers to underground operation to get food.

같이 화를 냈다.

세상이 달라졌다고 몇 번을 말해! 그냥 버리라니까!

이 귀한 걸 워치케 버린다냐. 쌀 한 톨 만들라고 농부들이 월매나 애를 쓰는디.

쌀이 남아도는 세상이야. 부지런히 먹고 버려줘야 농부들이 돈을 벌지.

딸이 아무리 말해도 그녀는 버리는 게 아깝다. 맛이야 어떻든 입에 들어가면 똑같다. 굶지 않으면 그만이다.

엄마. 엄마가 꿈꾸던 세상은 진즉에 이루어졌어. 여자들도 남자들과 똑같이 공부하지, 굶어 죽는 사람 없지. 뭐든 넘쳐서 문제인 세상이야. 그러니까 제발 좀 맛있는 것만 부지런히 먹으라구.

그녀도 그쯤은 안다. 동지들과 젊은 그녀가 목숨 바친 사상은 이미 막을 내렸다. 총 들고 싸웠던 자본주의가 세계 도처에 창궐하는데도 여자도 공부할 수 있고, 가난한 사람도 공부할 수 있는, 그녀가 꿈꾸는 세상이 되었다. 여자들이 뉴스에 나와 똑 부러지게 제 말 하는 것도 봤다. 그녀는 남편이 살아있다면 묻고 싶다.

우리가 뭣 땀시 그 고상을 했으까라?

남편은 죽는 날까지 희망을 잃은 적이 없는 사람이니

those bull parts!"

Pak's laughter is still ringing in her ears even without a hearing aid. Her comrades, who are ready to die and have lost nine other comrades in the morning battle, laugh a hearty laugh at a place that will be their graveyard. How strange it is. She has seen the faces of the dead clearly and brightly for some time. By contrast, the faces of the living look hazy and foggy. She has seen her daughter's friend this afternoon, but would not be able to recognize her face if she saw her again now. Her daughter's friend brought five boxes of snacks for her. She was told that they were pineapple cakes bought in Taiwan. They are the most delicious food that she has ever tasted in her life. It's been a long while since she lost her appetite, and she is so amused by the sweet taste that she eats one more cake. It seems to her that she has lived a long life to find the most delicious food at the age of ninety nine.

Since her daughter moved next door, she has tasted high-style dishes of every sort that she did not eat before. Pine mushrooms, scaly hedgehog mushrooms, abalones, oysters, clams, quahog clams, fried pork belly in soy sauce, and stir-fried seafood with vegetables. . . She is well aware that her daughter wants to treat her to the best food while she is alive, but having lost her appetite already, she prefers a simple bowl of soybean paste

아마 이렇게 답할 것이다.

우리가 그 고생을 했응게 시방 이만큼이라도 된 것이제 몰라 물어?

그녀는 모르겠다. 헛고생을 한 것인지, 눈곱만큼은 지금의 세상에 기여를 한 것인지. 곧 통일이 되고 평등한 세상이 될 거라고 확신하며 죽은 동지들이 부러울 때도 있다. 그때는 그녀에게도 세상이 명료했다. 목숨 바쳐 싸우면 더 좋은 세상이 될 거라고 믿어 의심치 않았다. 그녀가, 동지들이, 목숨 바쳐 싸우지 않았더라도 어쩌면 세상은 좋아지지 않았을까, 생각하면 힘이 빠진다. 이 세상에 설 자리가 없는 느낌이다. 세상의 밖으로 하염없이 밀려나는 기분, 모래사장의 한 알 모래가 된 기분, 산을 내려온 이래 늘 그런 기분으로 살았다. 딸아이가 태어나기 전까지는. 딸은 전에 그녀가 본 세상보다 한없이 작고 사소하지만, 그녀에게는 전부인 우주였다. 그 작은 행복에 취해 있다가 문득 지리산에서 바람이 불면 등골이 서늘해졌다. 이러라고, 이리 살라고, 수많은 동지들이 꽃 같은 목숨을 아낌없이 버렸던 것은 아닐 텐데…….

그마저도 오래전의 얘기다. 늙어 꼬부라진 몸, 세 발

soup to anything else. Only her eyes enjoy the luxury. The meals prepared by her daughter always remind her of her late husband. Having starved for ten days in the mountains, her husband passed out and collapsed on the ground on the way to a supply struggle. On the way back, his comrades broke a raw egg, for which a few of them had lost their lives, and spilled it in his unconscious mouth. The moment the egg reached his stomach, he opened his eyes. After that day, food was for him what gasoline was for a vehicle.

"Let's have gas at once."

He meant that it was time to eat. For her husband as well as those comrades who died in the mountains, food was gasoline that moved their bodies rather than something tasteful. Neither they nor she knew the fun of spending a lot of money for delicious food. That's how she lived. Her openhanded daughter cooks large enough portions every time, and promptly throws away the leftovers. If she secretly hides the leftovers to eat up in order not to waste them, her daughter will hit the roof.

"How many times have I told you that the world has changed? Throw them away!"

"How can I throw away such precious things? Farmers work like horses to produce a grain of rice."

"Rice is oversupplied these days. You had better eat it or throw it away as much as possible so that

걷기 어려운 몸, 뉴스를 봐도 반 이상 뭔 소린지 모르겠는 몸이다. 무엇을 했고 무엇을 이루었든, 죽은 몸이든 산 몸이든, 거기서 거기다.

밤이 깊어갈수록 어둠은 농밀해진다. 손을 뻗으면 어둠의 질감이 느껴진다. 솜이불처럼 두텁고 무거운 어둠이다. 모든 것을 삼킨 어둠은 죽음 그 자체 같기도 하다. 아침이 오고 빛이 스며들기 전까지 그녀는 죽음 속에 고요히 누워 있다. 죽은 것과 진배없는 그녀는 어둠 속에서 죽은 어머니를 만나고, 동생을 만난다. 아랫도리 벌거벗은 채 오롯한 몸의 쾌락에 탐닉해 있던 동생은 엎어놓은 사발 같은 단발머리를 하고 그녀 곁을 자꾸 맴돈다.

성! 성! 성!

어려서처럼 밤새 그녀의 잠으로도 찾아와 놀아달라고 옆구리를 질꺽거린다. 어머니의 죽음으로 세상에 온 동생이다. 그날 그녀에게 생과 사는 한 몸이었다. 어머니는 호롱불 아래 류충렬전을 소리 높여 읽고, 그녀는 동생의 기저귀를 간다. 달덩이처럼 보얀 동생의 엉덩이를 찰싹찰싹 두드린다. 동생이 꺄르르 웃는다.

방 밖으로 나가기 어려워지면서 그녀의 시간은 이 검

farmers can make money."

Whatever her daughter may say, she cannot waste food. Regardless of taste, the food is the same after she puts it in her mouth. The important thing is not to starve.

"Mom, the world you dreamed of has come true already. Women can study just like men, and nobody starves to death now. The problem is that everything is overflowing. So eat only the finest food, as much as possible."

That much she knows. The age of ideology, to which she and her comrades devoted their young lives, has come to an end. Despite their armed struggle, capitalism is still rampant throughout the world. Nonetheless, the world she dreamed of has come true, where women and the poor can study equally. She has seen independent and outspoken women on television news. She would like to ask her husband if he were still alive, "Why did we go through all those sufferings?"

Her husband never lost hope until his death, so he would probably answer like this: "The world has developed this much owing to our sufferings. Don't you know why?"

She does not know whether she made vain efforts or made a tiny contribution to the world of today. There are times when she envies her comrades who died with a firm belief in the imminent reunification

은 방에 갇혔다. 검은 방에서는 시간이 제 맘대로 흘러 죽은 자들이 살아 있고 함께 있을 수 없는 자들이 함께 있다. 직선으로 살아온 시간을 실타래처럼 엉켜놓은 것이 어둠인지 그녀 자신인지 알 수 없다. 검은 방에는 그녀의 구십구 년이 안개처럼 고여 있다. 그녀의 숨결에 따라 어떤 기억은 물 안개로 피어오르고 어떤 기억은 바닥으로 내려앉는다. 피어오르는 것은 묵은 기억들이다. 새로운 것들은 좀처럼 검은 방 안으로 스며들지 못한다. 날이 갈수록 검은 방의 기억들은 봄꽃처럼 찬란하게 피어난다. 그녀는, 살아있는 그녀는, 오직 기억 속에서만 살아있다.

어이, 가세. 멋 흐고 있능가. 후딱 나오제.

십삼 년 전 죽은 남편이다. 흉한 꼴 보이기 전에 제발 빨리 죽었으면 했던 남편이다. 죽은 남편이 그녀를 부른다. 그녀는 굼뜨게 일어나 어둠을 더듬거리며 나갈 채비를 한다.

후딱 나오랑게.

성미 급한 남편이 다그친다. 막 몸을 일으킨 침대 위, 몸 따라 일어나지 못한 그녀의 마음 한 자락 희끄무레 놓여 있다. 그 마음, 두꺼운 블라인드 너머, 딸의 방으로

of Korea that would lead to a fairer society. Back then, the world seemed clear to her, too. She had no doubt that a better world would come if she fought to the death. Thinking that the world would have probably become better even if she and her comrades had not fought to the death, she feels drained of energy. She feels like there is no place for her in this world. After she came down from the mountains, she always felt like she was endlessly pushed to the edge of the world, or reduced to a grain of sand on a beach. Then, her daughter was born. Compared to the world that she had seen before, her daughter was extremely small and insignificant, but soon became her whole universe. While she was lost in that small happiness, occasional winds from Jirisan sent chills down her spine. This kind of life could not have been the reason why numerous comrades had readily laid down their lives in the flower of their youth. . .

Even that was a long time ago. Now, she stoops with age, cannot walk more than three steps, and cannot understand half of the news programs. Whatever she has done or accomplished, whether her body is dead or alive, it's all the same.

As night deepens, darkness ripens. She reaches out her hand to feel the texture of darkness. It is as thick and heavy as a cotton-wool comforter. The

이어진다. 생생하게 살아 있던 아흔아홉 해의 기억들이 꿈이었던 듯 사라지고, 그녀는 우두커니, 저 따라나서지 않은 제 마음, 들여다본다. 그 마음, 치매 걸린 동생의 요분질과 다를 바 없다. 그런데도 그 마음, 거두어지지 않는다. 그녀는 검은 방, 구십구 년의 기억 속에 다시 갇힌다. 산 것인지 죽은 것인지, 기억들, 뒤엉켜 뛰논다.

all-devouring darkness seems to be death itself. She silently lies down in death until light comes into the room at the break of dawn. In a state no better than death, she meets her dead mother, and also her sister in darkness. Her sister, completely indulged in carnal pleasures, with naked buttocks, is lingering around the room with her hair bobbed like an upside-down bowl.

"Sis! Sis! Sis!"

Her sister comes to her sleep at night, poking her in the ribs and begging her to play with her, just like in childhood. Her sister came to this world through her mother's death. On the night of her sister's birth, life and death became one to her. Her mother is reading *The Tale of Ryu Chung-Yeol* aloud under a kerosene lamp, while she changes her sister's diapers. She playfully spanks her sister's buttocks as milky as the moon. Her sister gurgles with delight.

As she has grown too weak to step out of the room, her time is confined to this black room. In the black room, time goes by at its own pace, and thus, the dead are alive, while those who cannot be together are together. She does not know whether it is darkness or herself that has tangled up the time that she has linearly lived. Her ninety-nine years are veiled in mist in the black room. By her breath, some memories erupt to the surface as mist, while others settle to the bottom. The erupting memories are old ones. New ones can never pervade the black room. As days go by, memories in the black room bloom splendidly like spring flowers. She, who is alive, is alive only in memories.

"Hey, let's go! What keeps you so long? Come quickly!"

It is her husband who passed away thirteen years ago. She wanted him to die quickly, before he put himself to shame. Her dead husband calls her. She slowly sits up, and gropes through the darkness getting ready to go out.

"Come quickly!"

Her impatient husband pushes her. Having just raised herself off the bed, she finds a pale piece of her heart lying there, which has not followed her body yet. That piece of her heart extends to her daughter's place, beyond the thick window shade. Her vivid, living memories of ninety-nine years disappear as if they were just dreams, and vacantly, she stares at the heart that has not followed her. That heart is not different from the behavior of her senile sister mimicking sex. Yet, she cannot take it away. She is locked in the black room again, in the memories of ninety-nine years. Whether in life or in death, memories are romping around in a tangle.

창작노트
Writer's Note

박상륭 선생의 어머니는 쉰 넘어 선생을 낳았다. 어린 선생은 혹 늙은 어머니의 숨이 멎을까 불안해 잠들지 못했다. 자다가도 몇 번씩 깨어 어머니 심장이 뛰는지 확인할 정도였다. 죽음은 선생 문학의 화두가 되었다.

　내 어머니도 늙어 나를 낳았다. 요즘이야 마흔 넘어 출산하는 사람도 흔하지만 55년 전에는 거의 기적 같은 일이었다. 어머니는 몸이 약했고, 몇 번의 유산을 반복한 뒤였다. 나는 질기게도 탯줄에 매달려 열 달을 채웠다. 내가 젖을 빨면 속 창자까지 빨려 나오는 느낌이었다고, 그러니 약한 어미의 배 속에서 열 달을 버틸 수 있었던 거라고 늙은 어머니는 말하곤 했다. 어머니는 자

The writer, Park Sang-ryung's mother gave birth to him over the age of fifty. In childhood, he could not get to sleep for fear that his old mother's heart would stop beating. He woke up from his sleep several times every night to make sure that his mother's heart was still beating. Death became the main theme of his literary works.

My mother also gave birth to me at an old age. It is not uncommon for women over forty to have babies these days, but it was almost a miracle fifty-five years ago. She was weak after repeated miscarriages. I hung on to the umbilical cord tenaciously for ten months. According to my old mother, I sucked at her breast so hard that she felt like her intestines were sucked out, and thus, I could

주 아팠다. 아니, 늘 아팠다. 위가 좋지 않아 밥을 새 모이만큼 먹었고, 자주 위경련을 했고, 그러고 나면 일주일 가까이 곡기를 끊었다. 나는 어머니의 생명을 흡수해 살아가는 게 아닐까, 죄책감에 시달렸다. 그러거나 말거나 나는 씩씩하게 자라났고 어머니는 고달프게 늙어갔다. 그때부터 내 문학의 화두는 '늙음'이 아니었을까 싶다.

나는 쉰다섯이 되었고, 아프지 않은 때가 없었던 어머니는 팔순 넘어서도 어느 한 군데 아픈 데 없던 아버지를 먼저 보냈고, 그 뒤로도 시난고난 세월을 견디고 있다. 어머니 모신 지 여덟 해째다. 척추협착증을 앓는 어머니는 모시기 시작한 첫 몇 해 동안은 읍내 걸음도 간혹 했으나 차츰 행동반경이 좁아져 일 년째 문밖출입하지 않는다. 미장원 걸음도 끊었다. 자주 찾아오는, 손재주 좋은 내 제자가 어머니 전속 미용사다.

어머니는 밤에도 불을 켜지 않는다. 늙어 빛이 불편한 탓이라고 하지만 사실은 환하게 불을 밝히면 바깥이 보이지 않기 때문이다. 어머니가 말하는 바깥은 50미터쯤 떨어진 내 집이다. 어머니 집이 어두워야 환한 내 집이 잘 보인다. 어머니는 어둔 방에 갇혀 내가 환한 불빛 속

hold for ten months in the weak mother's womb. She was often sick, or rather, was always sick. She ate like a bird because of her weak stomach, having frequent stomach cramps, after which she stopped eating grains for almost a week. I felt guilty, wondering if my life was absorbing hers. Whether it was true or not, I grew up healthy and strong, while she grew old and weary. I guess, from then on, aging became my literary theme.

Now, I'm fifty-five years old, while my mother, who was always ill, survived my father who had perfect health past the age of eighty. She has barely endured time until today. Eight years have passed since I began to support her. Suffering from spinal stenosis, she used to go to town once in a while for the first few years after I moved next door to her. Gradually, however, the range of her activities has narrowed, and she has not stepped out of her house for over a year. She does not go to a hair salon anymore. Now, her hairdresser, a dextrous student of mine, pays frequent visits to us.

My mother does not turn on the light even at night. Her excuse is that the light irritates her old eyes, but the real reason is that she cannot look outside the window with the light on. To her, 'outside' means my house at a fifty-meter distance. She keeps her place dark in order to see my house lit up. Locked up in her dark room, she continues

에서 이리저리 움직이는 것을 보고 또 본다. 나는 어머니의 우주다.

한때 내 어머니는 총명한 사회주의자였다. 조국 통일을 위해 기꺼이 목숨을 걸었던 용맹한 전사이기도 했다. 아버지 살아있을 때만 해도 어머니는 아홉 시 뉴스의 열렬한 시청자였고, 구례의 온갖 선거에 관여하는 정치꾼이었다. 아버지의 죽음과 함께 어머니의 세상은 서서히 닫혔고, 이제 어머니는 세 평 남짓, 검은 방에 갇혔다.

아무것도 하지 않는 어머니의 시간이 궁금했다. 어머니는 아침 열 시, 저녁 여섯 시, 하루 두 끼를 정확한 시간에 먹는다. 그 사이 와이티엔 뉴스를 보고, 초등학교 시절의 내 일기나 감옥에 있던 아버지와 우리 모녀가 주고받은 편지를 골백번 읽는다. 오륙 년 전만 해도 어머니는 무언가를 잔뜩 적어놓았다가 묻곤 했다.

에프티에이가 뭐냐?

포쥐가 뭐냐?

어머니의 궁금증은 나날이 줄어들었다. 이제는 더 이상 아무것도 묻지 않는다. 세상에 아무런 호기심도 생기지 않는 것이다. 어머니의 유일한 현재는 나다. 그마

to stare at me moving here and there in the bright light. I am her universe.

Once, my mother was a smart socialist. She was also a brave warrior who would readily lay down her life for the sake of national reunification. Before my father's death, she was an ardent viewer of the news as well as a politician involved in all elections in Gurye. With his death, however, her world was gradually closed, and now, she is locked up in the ten-square-meter black room.

I was curious about how my mother spent her days doing nothing. She eats two meals at the exact time everyday; breakfast at 10:00 a.m. and dinner at 6:00 p.m. In the interval, she watches the YTN news, and reads my diaries from elementary school or letters between my father, who was in prison at that time, and us a hundred times. Five or six years ago, she used to write down many memos to ask me about them.

"What is the FTA?"

"What is 4G?"

Her curiosity decreased day by day. Now, she does not ask anything anymore. She has no curiosity about the world. Her only present is me. Even that is too much for her to remember. Last year, she memorized almost all of my lecturing days and the college names where I taught. This year, she asks me about them every week.

저도 점점 기억하지 못한다. 작년만 해도 어머니는 내가 강의 나가는 요일과 대학 이름을 거의 외웠다. 올부터는 매주 묻는다.

조대 간다고 했냐? 몇 시에 오냐?

어머니가 그마저도 묻지 않게 될까 두렵다.

어머니의 삶에서 가장 먼저 미래가 사라졌다. 일 년 뒤나 십 년 뒤나 어머니의 일상은 변하지 않을 것이고, 하여 어머니는 죽을 날 외에는 관심이 없다. 그리고 이제 현재가 사라지고 있다. 어머니의 시간을 지배하는 것은 과거다. 밥을 먹다 말고 어머니의 시간은 뜬금없이 먼 옛날로 뜀뛰기를 한다. 밤마다 류충렬전을 읽던 외할머니, 공부는 관심 밖이요, 밥하고 수놓는 것만 좋아라 하던 귀남이 이모, 구례서 처음으로 토마토를 심었다는 첫 남편, 너무 잘생겨 모든 여자들이 홀렸다는 박종하, 대학 시절부터 수백 번은 더 들은 이야기들이다.

한 사람에게 기억되는 인생의 장면이 총 얼마나 될까? 어머니의 이야기는 타원형처럼 여기에서 거기로, 거기에서 여기로 맴돈다. 세월이 흐르면서 어머니의 이야기는 조금씩 살이 붙어 저절로 자라난다. 그건 사실이 아니라고 아무리 항변해도 어머니는 내 말보다 자신

"Are you going to Joseon University today? What time are you coming back?"

I fear that she will stop asking at all some day.

In my mother's life, the first thing that disappeared was the future. Her daily life will not change whether in a year or in ten years, so nothing interests her but the day that she will die. And now, the present is disappearing. Her time is ruled by the past. Dinner is abruptly interrupted when her time suddenly jumps to the remote past. My maternal grand-mother would read *The Tale of Ryu Chung-Yeol* every night, my aunt Guinam detested studying and loved cooking and embroidery, my mother's first husband planted tomatoes for the first time in Gurye, and Pak Jong-ha was so handsome that he enchanted all women. These are the stories that I have heard several hundred times since my college days.

How many scenes could one remember in life? My mother's stories are circling around in the same place, like being caught in a net. As years go by, her stories spontaneously grow up little by little. No matter how hard I protest that it is not true, she trusts her memories rather than my words. Sometimes, I think that memories may not be dead things. The memories embedded in her mind may have grown by themselves over the years, so as to live at another level of time different from that of the real mother.

My mother's black room is a place where her

의 기억을 믿는다. 때로 나는 생각한다. 기억은 죽어 있
는 것이 아닐지도 모른다고. 어머니의 머릿속에 각인된
기억들은 세월 속에 절로 자라, 실재의 어머니와는 또
다른 차원의 시간을 살고 있는지도 모른다고.

　어머니의 검은 방은 한평생의 기억이 실타래처럼 풀
려나온, 그러니까 구십사 년의 시간이 입체로 고여 있
는 곳이다. 그중 어떤 기억들을 붙잡고 어머니는 어떤
시간들을 살아내고 있다. 그러니까 어머니의 검은 방은
어머니가 살아온 세상이며, 살아야 할 이유이며, 동시
에 죽어도 상관없는 이유기도 하다. 누구의 끝인들, 어
머니의 검은 방이 기다리고 있지 않겠는가. 사람은 그
렇게 제가 살아온 한 세상을 소처럼 되새기고 되새겨,
아무리 사소한 인생이었다 할지라도 그 사소한 기억에
불멸성을 입힌 후에야, 비로소 무거운 생명을 내려놓고
무로 화하든가, 천국이든 극락이든 또 다른 세상으로
건너뛸 수 있는 것일지 모른다.

　어머니가 가고 나도 나는 오래 어머니의 검은 방을
잊지 못할 것 같다. 어머니가 가도 그 방에는 어머니의
한평생이 고여 있을 것 같아서다.

　나는 요즘 어딘가를 본다. 창 너머 지리산이든, 어머

lifelong memories unravel like a thread, that is, where her ninety-four years' time lingers in a three-dimensional pool. She is living in a certain time by clinging to certain memories. Her black room is, therefore, the world that she has lived, her reason to live, and at the same time, her reason to die at any time. Who can avoid the black room waiting for us at the end of our lives? We may have to look back on the lifetime we have lived over and over, like a cow chews her cud, in order to endow immortality on trivial memories, however trivial our lives may have been. Only then, we may lay down our heavy lives and turn into nothingness, or jump into another world, be it heaven or nirvana.

If my mother passes away, it won't be easy for me to forget her black room for a long time, since her whole life will be lingering in the room even in her absence.

These days, I often stare at some places. Whether it is Jirisan Mountain outside the window, or my mother's black room, or the space between my students sitting side by side, these places are not empty. There, the memories of someone's muddy, hard and stumbling life are immortalized and floating in the air. Someday, my own memories will probably float in a certain space, too.

Born to an elderly mother, I am also growing old. Since I still have the present, my old memories do

니의 검은 방이든, 학생과 학생이 앉아있는 의자 사이든 그곳들은 비어있지 않다. 그곳엔 누군가의 질척거렸던, 비틀거렸던, 신산했던 한 삶의 기억이 불멸의 것으로 화하여 부유하고 있다. 언젠가는 나의 기억도 어떤 공간을 떠돌고 있을지 모른다.

늙은 어머니에게서 태어난 내가 늙어가고 있다. 나에겐 아직 현재가 있어 묵은 기억들이 실타래처럼 풀려나오지 않는다. 하지만 기억으로 축적되는 것들이 줄어들고 있는 것을 느낀다. 오십오 년을 살며 어지간한 일에는 내성이 생겨 어지간해서는 기억으로 축적되지 않는 것이다.

늙어간다는 것은 쓸쓸하다. 그러나 두렵지는 않다. 나의 늙음이 아니라 어머니의 늙음을 지켜보는 일이 두렵다. 나의 늙음은 스스로 감당하면 될 일, 내게 생명을 준 자, 이제는 아이처럼 천진해진 어머니가 늙어가는 모습을 지켜보는 일은 참담하다. 이것이 사랑인가? 모르겠다. 다만 도무지 초연해지지 않는다.

오늘도 어머니의 방은 어둡다. 어머니는 지금 어느 시간을 살고 있는 것일까?

not unravel like a thread. Yet, I feel that less and less things are stored in my memory. Having lived for fifty-five years, I have developed tolerance for a lot of things, and now, it is quite difficult for anything to be held in my memory.

Growing old feels lonely, but does not scare me. I'm not afraid of my aging, but afraid of seeing my mother aging. I can cope with my own aging, but feel terrible to see my mother, who gave me life, growing old and childlike. Is this love? I do not know. I just cannot remain undisturbed.

Tonight, my mother's room is dark as always. What kind of time is she living in now?

해설
Commentary

좀처럼, 끝나지 않는 전투

정은경 (문학평론가)

「검은 방」의 이야기는 30년 전부터 시작되었다. 89년 스물 다섯의 작가가 실록 소설인 『빨치산의 딸』을 《실천문학》에 연재했을 때부터 「검은 방」의 '그녀'는, '이옥자'(『빨치산의 딸』)는 산에서 내려와 우리와 함께 살기 시작했다고 할 수 있다. 그러나 목숨 걸고 산에서 싸웠던 '지리산의 영웅들'이 산에서 내려온 후 어떻게 살았는지에 대해서는 풍문으로 들었을 뿐 잘 알지 못한다. 그저 그들의 처절한 싸움은 산 위에서 끝났고, 우리와 다르지 않은 지리멸렬한 일상으로 흩어졌을 뿐이라고 짐작할 뿐. 그러나 그들의 전투는 토벌의 끝자락인 1954년에도, 그리고 『빨치산의 딸』이 세상에 출간된 1990년에

The Battle That Never Ends

Jung Eun-kyoung (Literary critic)

The story of *The Black Room* began 30 years ago. In
1989, the then twenty-five-year-old author's
nonfiction novel titled *The Daughter of Partisans* was
serialized in the literary quarterly *Silcheonmunhak*.
Along with its publication, 'she' in *The Black Room*,
named Yi Ok-ja in *The Daughter of Partisans*, came
down from the mountains to live with us. Regarding
the 'heroes of Jirisan Mountain' who fought with
their lives, little is known about their lives after they
left Jirisan, apart from some rumors. One can only
presume that they eventually scattered in tedious
daily life, like the rest of us, after their desperate
struggle had ended in Jirisan. Their battle, however,
did not stop either at the end of the government's
suppression in 1954, nor with the publication of *The*

도 끝나지 않았다. 지리산의 '지'와 백아산의 '아'에서 비롯된 이름이 상징하듯, '정지아'와 그의 부모는 '빨치산'의 운명에 씌어진 길고 긴 전투를 여전히 치러내고 있는 중이다.

작가 정지아는 남로당 전남도당 인민위원장이었던 아버지와 여맹위원장이었던 어머니를 둔 '빨치산의 딸'이다. 작가 정지아가 마주한 인생의 첫 싸움은 초등학교 4학년 "느그 아부지가 빨갱이람서?"라는 친구의 도발로 시작된다. 이 낙인으로 인해 세상과 단절하고 책 속에 파묻힌 어린 소녀는 커서 작가가 되었고, 빨치산 이야기를 꺼내놓았으나 '이적표현물'로 판매금지 당한다. 몇 년간 수배자로 도피 생활을 하고 집행유예를 받고 하는 동안 세상은 바뀌어 그녀는 등단 작가가 되었고, 봉인된 이야기도 2005년 복간되어 세상에 풀려난다. 그러나 「검은 방」에 적힌 것처럼 '빨치산의 딸'이라는 표식은 끝내 그녀를 제도권 밖으로, 그녀와 그녀의 부모를 '산'으로 밀어낸다. 인적 드문 그곳, 지리산의 컴컴한 어둠 속에서 벌어지는, 좀처럼 끝나지 않는 이들의 전투를 담은 이야기가 「검은 방」이다.

「검은 방」의 주인공은 아흔아홉 살의 노파이다. 그녀

Daughter of Partisans in book form in 1990. Symbolized by the author's first name, Ji-a, which is an acronym from the mountains of Jiri and Baeg-A, Jeong Ji-a and her parents are still fighting the long-lasting battle, carrying the fate of the partisans.

Jeong Ji-a is the 'daughter of partisans'; her father was Deputy Head of Organization Department (Chair of the People's Committee) in the Jeonnam Provincial Party Committee of the South Korean Labor Party, while her mother was a political instructor (Chair of the Women's League) of the Southern Army. As a fourth-grader in elementary school, the author engaged in the very first fight in her life, which started with a friend's provocation that the author's father was a 'commie.' Shutting herself off from the world and immersed in reading, the stigmatized girl grew up to be a writer to publish the story of partisans, but her book was banned for 'aiding and abetting the enemy.' She had been on the wanted list for a few years until she was sentenced to probation. Meanwhile, the world had changed, and she became an acclaimed writer, with her banned story republished in 2005. As written in *The Black Room*, however, the stigma of the partisans' daughter drove her out of the mainstream, pushing her and her parents to a remote village in Jirisan. In that desolate place, in the pitch darkness of the mountain, the story of their never-ending battle

는 『빨치산의 딸』의 '이옥자'처럼 남편과 함께 지리산에 입산하여 남부군으로 싸우다 남편과 동지들을 잃고 체포되어 5년간 감옥살이를 한다. 감옥에서 나와 허허벌판에 던져진 그녀는 동지였던 한 남자를 만나 안착하게 되고, 마흔둘에 딸아이를 낳으면서 뿌리를 내리게 된다. 사상을 잃은 뒤 '단 하나의 현재'이자 삶의 이유가 된 딸을 등대 삼아 그녀와 남편은 서툰 농삿일을 하고 허리가 굽도록 밤을 주우면서 늙어간다. 그렇게 늙어가는 동안 딸은 대학을 졸업하고 결혼을 하고 자식을 낳으며 '무던하게' 살아낸다. 그리고 이제 '늙어버린 어미'는 노심초사 길러낸 딸의 유일한 걱정거리가 된다. 치매를 앓던 아버지가 죽자 딸은 계약직 교수를 그만두고 홀로 있는 지리산의 어머니 곁으로 내려와 그녀를 돌본다. 첫 남편과 동지들, 치매 걸린 남편을 떠나보낼 때마다 "금방 따라갈라요. 먼저 가서 자리 잡고 있으씨요이"라던 그녀의 다짐은 또다시 딸이 거처하는 윗집의 등불에 붙들리고 만다.

얼핏 보면 「검은 방」은 빨치산 경력을 지닌 노모와 딸의 일상을 담은 이야기지만, 작가가 전하는 이들의 삶 곳곳에는 핏빛 진달래와 같은 처절한 전투가 새겨져

unfolds in *The Black Room*.

The Black Room's protagonist is a ninety-nine-year-old woman. Just like Yi Ok-ja in *The Daughter of Partisans*, she entered Jirisan with her husband to join the Southern Army, lost her husband and other comrades, and was captured to serve a five-year prison term. Released from prison, she had nowhere to turn to, but settled down by marrying an ex-comrade, and finally got her feet on the ground by giving birth to her daughter at the age of forty two. After she gave up the fight for her beliefs, her daughter became the 'only present' as well as her only reason to live, like a lighthouse for her. She and her husband did farm work that was strange and strenuous for them, and picked chestnuts until they became stooped from work. While she grew old, her daughter graduated from college, got married, and had a child, 'without making any trouble.' The 'elderly mother' then becomes her daughter's only worry, whom she has raised with all her energy. After the death of her senile husband, her daughter quits her job as an adjunct professor, and moves next door to her in order to take care of her living alone in Jirisan. "I will follow you soon. Go first and wait for me!," said she when she survived her first husband, other comrades and her senile husband. Yet, her promise is withheld again by the light from her

있다. 감옥에서 풀려난 '그녀'가 맞닥뜨린 첫 번째 전투는, 동지들과 목숨 걸고 싸웠던 '친일청산과 조국통일' 같은 구호가 더 이상 허용되지 않는 세상과의 타협이다. 달라진 세상에서 '젊은 빨갱이년'은 남정네들의 욕정의 대상으로 전락하고, '산에서 죽었어야 한다'고 입술을 깨물며 치욕을 견디던 그녀는 빨치산 동지를 만나 딸아이를 낳고 또 다른 전투를 치르게 된다. 그녀가 불러낸 생명을 품고 키우는 일.

이 평범한 일이 빨갱이 전력을 가진 이들 가족에게는 빨치산의 그것 못지않은 전투를 의미한다. 왜냐하면 길고 긴 생이란 이데올로기에 대한 신념과 혁명적 낙관주의처럼 '명료하고 산뜻한 것'이 아니기 때문에. 배고프고 졸리고 아픈 몸은 지리산의 전사들에게 끝없이 모욕과 굴욕을 강요한다. 그러나 그 모욕 앞에서 새끼를 품은 어미는 한없이 굴종할 수밖에 없다. 사상을 잃은 자리에 이제 딸은 세상의 중심이 되어 '그녀'의 삶을 이끈다.

지리산 산골의 '검은 방'은 그렇게 살아낸 아흔아홉의 몸이 적멸을 향해가는 공간이지만, 어둠으로 가득 찬 이곳에는 적막 대신 최후의 격전지처럼 여전히 소요와 격정으로 들끓는다. 근처 대학에 출강하는 딸의 귀가와

daughter's house next door.

At first glance, *The Black Room* is a story about the everyday life of an ex-partisan elderly mother and her daughter, but all aspects of their lives represent their desperate battles as blood-red as azaleas. In the first battle that 'she' faced after the release from prison, she had to compromise with a society that had stopped calling for the punishment of pro-Japanese Koreans and reunification, for which she and her comrades had laid down their lives. In the changed society, the 'young commie bitch' fell so low as to be the object of lustful desire. She suffered disgrace biting her lips, regretting that she had not died in the mountains. Then, she met an ex-comrade, gave birth to her daughter, and began another battle of raising a child she had given life to.

To her family with a partisan past, such an ordinary thing meant a battle as rigorous as partisans' struggle, since her long life was not as 'lucid and fresh' as her faith in socialism and revolutionary optimism. Being hungry, tired and sick, the warrior of Jirisan was forced to endure constant insults and humiliation. Faced with humiliation, however, the mother embracing a child could not but surrender over and over. In place of ideology, her daughter becomes the center of her world to lead her life now.

The 'black room' in the mountain village is a place

방의 불빛이 밝아지기를 초조하게 기다리는 노모의 감각 주변에는 지리산의 먼 기억과 가까운 과거가 동시다발적으로 날아오른다.

그 기억 속에는 남편이 죽은 뒤 그녀를 돌봐주던 박종하의 죽음과 그의 수의를 짓던 서른의 그녀가 있고, 또 남부군에 순경인 남편을 잃고도 박종하를 연모해 좇아나선 소복 입은 철없는 처자도 있다. 그리고 그 젊은 처자를 경멸하던 그녀의 차가운 눈은 "살아도 살아도 모르겠는 세상, 그러지 말 것을 서러운 등짝 한 번 가만히 쓸어줄 것을, 그 가만한 손길로 어쩌면 사랑에 미친 제 죄를 용서받은 양 한평생 견뎌냈을지도 모를 것을"이라는 회한과 함께 섞인다.

'검은 방'의 먼지처럼 떠오르는 기억 속에는 지리산의 일을 '사랑의 밀어'처럼 나누며 함께 했던 두 번째 남편과의 일생이, 그리고 양갈래 머리로 촐랑거리는 딸애의 모습과 딸의 등록금을 마련하기 위해 밤껍질을 벗기던 겨울밤이 있다. 그리고 밤을 까던 그 밤에 남편이 부르던 "태백산맥에 눈 내린다./총을 들어라 출정이다"라는 출정가는 다시 토벌대에 쫓겨 폭설이 내리는 천왕봉 아래 눈구덩이에서 몸을 숨기고 며칠을 굶던 그 밤의 나

where the ninety-nine-year-old body is on the way to annihilation. Full of darkness but far from being silent, the place is still filled with disturbance and passion, like the last ferocious battlefield. The elderly mother is impatiently waiting for her daughter, a lecturer at a nearby university, to come home, and for her daughter's house to be lit, while memories of the remote past in Jirisan and those of the recent past fly through her mind simultaneously.

In those memories, Pak Jong-ha, who took care of her after her husband's death, was killed in action, and she is sewing his shroud at the age of thirty, while an imprudent young woman in white mourning clothes is wailing for Pak, who fell for him even after having lost her policeman husband during the Southern Army's attack. Now, her cold eyes that used to despise the young woman are mixed with regret: "The world remains incomprehensible no matter how long she lives, so she should not have done it, but instead, should have gently patted the grieving woman on the back. Her gentle hands could have helped the woman endure life, as if she had been forgiven her sin of falling crazy in love."

Memories rise like dust in the black room, showing her life with her second husband who whispered with her about their struggle in Jirisan, like lovers' whispers. They also show her daughter cheerfully running around with her long hair

지막한 출정가에 겹쳐진다.

검은 방에는 또 이념을 위해 목숨을 걸었던, '퍼렇게 날 선 한 자루 검'과 같은 젊은 날의 그녀와 아랫목의 갱엿처럼 녹아내린 늙은 그녀가 함께 있다. "나흘이나 쌀한 톨 먹지 못한 채 차가운 동굴의 물속에 몸을 숨기고 있을 때, 코앞으로 지나가는 국군의 무리를 피해 숨을 죽일 때" 그런 것이 살아있는 것이라 믿었던 투사 여맹위원장은 이제 딸이 출강하는 수요일과 목요일에 동그라미를 쳐놓고 하염없이 밖을 내다보는 늙은 그녀와 함께 딸을 기다리는 중이다.

그 기다림 속에서 지리산에서 열흘 굶은 남편이 보급투쟁을 나갔다가 정신을 잃고 달걀을 먹고 깨어났을 때의 일과 음식이 아까워 버리지 못하고 몰래 먹는 그녀에게 "세상이 달라졌다고 몇 번을 말해! 그냥 버리라니까!"라고 호통치는 딸의 얼굴이 격투한다. "쌀이 남아도는 세상이야. 부지런히 먹고 버려줘야 농부들이 돈을 벌지. (…) 엄마가 꿈꾸던 세상은 진즉에 이루어졌어. 여자들도 남자들과 똑같이 공부하지, 굶어죽는 사람 없지. 뭐든 넘쳐서 문제인 세상이야."라는 딸의 이야기에 총 들고 싸웠던 자본주의가 부린 요술에 놀라 "우리가

meticulously braided on both sides, as well as one winter night when she and her husband peeled off dried shells of chestnuts to pay her daughter's college tuition. That night, her husband sang a military song; "Snow falls in the Taebaek Mountains. Take your guns! It's time for war!" That night overlaps with another night in Jirisan when the same song was lowly sung by partisans on the run, hiding in snow caves under Cheonwangbong Peak and starving for days in heavy snow.

Furthermore, the thirty-year-old who risked her life for socialism like a 'sharp-bladed sword' and the ninety-nine-year-old who has melted down like a 'piece of mushy taffy on a hot floor' coexist in the black room. "When hiding in a cold watery cave without eating a grain of rice for four days, when holding her breath to avoid a bunch of ROK soldiers marching right in front of her," she believed that was the way to live. Now, the former warrior checks every Wednesday and Thursday in red on her calendar, which are her daughter's lecturing days, and looks out the window blankly, waiting for her daughter.

While waiting for her daughter, she recalls a day when her husband, having starved for ten days in Jirisan, passed out on the way to a supply struggle, but regained consciousness after eating a raw egg. This is contrasted with her daughter storming at

뭣 땀시 그 고상을 했을까라?"라고 허망해하는 그녀가
또 전투를 벌인다.

그 뒤를 이어 '치매'에 걸린 남편을 삼 년 동안 수발하
던 그녀와 치매에 걸린 여동생의 마지막 모습이 따른
다. 요양원에서 만난 늙은 여동생이 사람도 알아보지
못하고 엉덩이를 들썩이며 요분질하던 모습은 동생을
낳자마자 죽은 어머니의 기억과 어린 동생의 보얀 궁둥
이와 섞인다. 열다섯에 땅꾼에게 시집가서 일찍 죽은
제부 대신 홀로 네 아이를 키워낸 동생의 마지막 모습
에 충격과 모욕을 느낀 그녀는 치매 앓는 남편이 딸 자
식에게 짐이 될까봐 쥐약이든 농약이든 먹고 죽자 결심
하고 겨울 지리산에 나선다. 그러나 지리산의 매서운
바람이 그녀의 걸음을 방해한다. '영하 사십 도를 훌쩍
넘는 한겨울에도 누더기에 짚신 차림 거침없이 헤쳐가
던' 그녀이건만 봄밤 훈풍과도 같은 바람에 가로막혀 주
저앉고 만다. 그 속에서 바람의 속삭임을 듣는다. "우리
맹꺼정 다 엎어줬웅게 원 없이 살다오시게"라는, 죽은
자들의 소리를.

그러나 죽은 자들이 남긴 "실컨 사씨요. 죽을 때꺼정
사씨요"라는 말이 축복인지 형벌인지 그녀는 알 수 없

her, when she secretly eats up the leftovers not to waste them; "How many times have I told you that the world has changed? Throw them away!" "Rice is oversupplied these days. You had better eat it or throw it away as much as possible so that farmers can make money." "Mom, the world you dreamed of has come true already. Women can study just like men, and nobody starves to death now. The problem is that everything is overflowing." Startled by her daughter's words and also by the magic of capitalism that she fought with guns, she engages in another battle, lamenting, "Why did we go through all those sufferings?"

It is followed by the memories of her senile husband, whom she looked after for three years, and the last encounter with her younger sister who also went senile. The image of her senile sister lifting her pelvis and mimicking sex in a nursing home without recognizing her is mixed with the memory of her deceased mother who died at childbirth, and also with the image of her infant sister's milky buttocks. At the age of fifteen, her sister was married off to a snake hunter, who died an untimely death, and raised four children by herself. The last glimpse of her sister shocks and insults her so much that she decides that she and her senile husband should die together, either by rat poison or by pesticide, so as not to burden her

다. 생의 모호함과 비정과 치욕이 칼날처럼 선명하고 숭고한 죽음보다 낫다고 할 수 없기 때문이다. 그녀가 동지들을 보내고 살아낸 생은 그녀에게 진리의 밝은 빛과 간명한 깨달음 대신 차라리 더 지독한 무명과 혼돈을 남겨준다. "한여름 뙤약볕처럼 수그러들 줄 모르는 생명"의 뻔뻔한 욕망에 대한 지독한 환멸과 경악, 그러나 어느 순간 그 존재가 기적과 경이로움으로 탈바꿈하는 블랙홀 같은 곳이 그녀의 검은 방이다.

이 격렬한 전투가 벌어지는 「검은 방」은 그러나 무겁거나 어둡지 않다. 그녀의 '검은 방'에는 고통과 절망과 패배가 어둠 속에 가라앉지 않고, 환희와 사랑과 행복이 날아오르지 않는다. 이 모든 정념을 입은 기억들은 그녀의 '검은 방'에서 푸가의 화음처럼 서로를 비추면서 아름답게 울려퍼진다. 깊은 통찰력을 거쳐나온 작가의 '눈송이' 같은 경쾌한 삶의 태도가 이 전투들을 다음과 같은 시적인 감각으로 변형시켜놓기 때문이다.

엄마!

꿈인지 생시인지 딸이 그녀를 부른다. 살짝 들춘 블라인드 너머, 긴 머리를 야무지게 양 갈래로 묶은 딸애

daughter. Then, she hits the road in winter, but her steps are hindered by the harsh wind from Jirisan. "Even when the temperature had fallen to forty degrees below zero in midwinter, she and her comrades in rags and straw shoes had crisscrossed the mountain," but now, she cannot move forward against the wind that is merely a warm spring breeze. There, she listens to the whisper of the wind, the voice of the dead; "We gave you our share of life, so please live as long as you wish before you come back to us!"

The dead say, "Please live as long as you wish! Live as long as you breathe!" Yet, she does not know whether it is a blessing or a punishment, since she cannot tell that the ambiguous, cruel and shameful life is better than a sublime death as sharp as a sword. Her long life, in which she survived many comrades, has led her to even worse ignorance and chaos, rather than to the bright light of truth and simple enlightenment. She is utterly appalled and disillusioned by the shameless desire of life, which is like "the scorching midsummer sun that would never die down," but at a certain point, that thing turns into a miracle and wonder in the black hole of her black room.

The black room, where those fierce battles take place, is nevertheless neither heavy nor dark. In the black room, her pain, despair and defeat do not settle

가 보인다. 화장실에 가려는 참이었는지 딸 손에 손전등이 들려 있다. 딸이 전등을 하늘로 비춘다. 하얀 눈송이가 빛기둥 안에 갇힌다. 아이 주먹만 한 눈송이들이 빛 아래서 한 점의 흔들림도 없이 고요히 내려앉는다. 하늘과 땅 사이를 가득 메운 눈송이가 열일곱 소녀의 마음을 뒤흔들어 딸은 아무도 밟지 않은 순결한 눈밭을 방방 뛰어다닌다. 딸의 움직임에 따라 갈래머리가 봄날 흰싸리밭의 나비처럼 나풀거린다. 캉캉, 흰 진돗개 똑순이가 딸의 뒤를 좇아 껑충껑충 뛴다. (24쪽)

열일곱 딸이 만든 빛 속에서 눈송이가 춤을 추고, 딸의 갈래머리가 봄날 나비처럼 나풀거리고, 진돗개가 껑중껑중 뛰는 이 아름다운 장면은 '검은 방'의 전투를 장식하는 궁극의 선율이자 어둠 속에서 날아오르는 뜻밖의 에피파니이다. 그 속에서 죽음과 생은 경계를 넘고 산 자와 죽은 자, 빛과 어둠, 숭고와 치욕, 환희와 고통, 기쁨과 슬픔이 용서나 속죄, 참회와 단죄 없이 하나가 된다.

가벼운 것이 농밀한 어둠 속에 무겁게 내려앉고 무거운 것이 햇살 속에 날아오르기도 하는 이 검은 방의 마

into darkness, while her joy, love and happiness do not fly into the sky, either. Revealed by all these feelings, her memories beautifully resonate with one another, as if in a harmonious fugue, in the black room. Reflecting a deep insight, the author's attitude toward life is as light as 'snowflakes,' and transforms the battles into a poetic scene as follows:

"Mom!"

Her daughter calls her as if in a dream. Or is it reality? Through the slightly lifted shade, she sees her daughter with her long hair meticulously braided on both sides. Presumably on the way to the outhouse, her daughter is holding a flashlight in her hand. She shines her flashlight up into the sky. White snowflakes are caught in a pole of light. Snowflakes as big as babies' fists are falling down straightforward and silent in the light. Enchanted by the great snowflakes filling the space between the sky and the earth, the seventeen-year-old girl is cheerfully running around the innocent snowfield that has not been stepped on. Along with her steps, her braided hair flutters like butterflies in a white bush clover field in spring. "Bowwow," a white Jindo dog named Smartie happily jumps around her daughter.

Snowflakes are dancing in the pole of light made by her seventeen-year-old daughter, and her

술은, 사실 아흔아홉의 '그녀'가 보고 있는 건너편 딸의 방 불빛에서 풀려나온 것이다. 검은 방의 '그녀' 앞에 죽은 남편과 동지들이 이 끊임없이 유혹하며 "후딱 나오제"라고 속삭여도, 그녀는 '몸 따라 일어나지 못한다.' 왜냐하면 검은 방 가득 메운 과거와 기억은 그녀가 하염없이 기다리는 딸이라는 '단 하나의 현재'를 이기지 못하기 때문이다. 하여 아흔아홉의 그녀는 죽은 자를 따라나서지 못하고 그녀를 이끄는 '마음 한 자락'에 끌려 주저앉는다. 치매걸린 동생이 요분질하던 그 마음과 다를 바 없다는 그 '마음'이란 '욕망'이라 아무리 낮추어 말할지라도 사실, 죽음과 욕망을 이기는 사랑을 의미한다. 한 존재를 향한 어떤 마음이 살아서 마주해야할 온갖 모욕과 허망을 기꺼이 감내하게 만든다. 그러므로 '검은 방'에서 딸을 기다리며 좀처럼, 끝나지 않는 마지막 전투를 치르는 그녀의 마음이란 살아있는 것을 살아있게 하는 마음, 지리산에서 싸우던 그 마음이며 일상의 전투를 치러내는 우리의 마음이기도 하다. '검은 방' 아흔아홉 구비의 산맥을 넘나드는 그녀의 끝없는 전투는 무명의 매일 속에서 '너'를 위해 살아가는 우리들의 전투이기도 한 것이다.

daughter's braided hair flutters like butterflies in spring, while a dog is jumping around her. This beautiful scene is the ultimate tune decorating the battle in the black room, and also an unexpected epiphany rising from darkness. In the black room, there is no boundary between life and death; the dead and the living, light and darkness, sublimity and disgrace, joy and pain, and happiness and sorrow become one without forgiveness and atonement, or without repentance and punishment.

In the black room, light things heavily descend in the dense darkness, while heavy things fly in sunshine, and in fact, this magic comes from the light from her daughter's house next door that she sees at the age of ninety nine. Her dead husband and comrades whisper to her, "Come quickly!," constantly seducing her to get out of the black room, but her heart does not follow her body. The reason is that the past and her memories filling the black room cannot beat the 'only present,' which is her daughter whom she is ceaselessly waiting for. At the age of ninety nine, therefore, she cannot follow the dead, but instead, is pulled back by a 'piece of her heart.' That heart, which is not different from the heart of her senile sister mimicking sex, is looked down on as 'desire.' As a matter of fact, however, that heart is love that beats death and desire. Love makes the heart, devoted to another being, readily endure all kinds of insults and untruth that one has to face in life. In consequence, her heart, waiting for her daughter and engaging in the last and never-ending battle in the black room, is the same heart that fought in the mountains and keeps living things alive. It is also the same heart as ours that engages in the wars of daily life. Her endless battle in the ninety-nine corners of the mountain in the black room is also our own battle, who live humble lives devoted to 'you.'

비평의 목소리
Critical Acclaim

사람들의 시선을 받지 않아도 늘 제자리를 지키며 제 몫의 잎사귀와 열매를 맺는 고욤나무는 힘없고 보잘 것 없는 존재들에게도 자기 몫의 생이 있으며 그것 자체만으로도 찬란하고 아름다울 수 있음을 환기한다. 이렇듯 정지아 소설에 등장하는 인물들은 고욤나무처럼 그 존재가 미미하지만 오랜 세월을 견디면서 자기 몫의 생을 살아가는 윤리적 감각을 갖춘 인물들이다. 또한 그들은 심해의 물고기가 "납작한 몸과 퇴화된 눈으로 어둠에 잠겨" 있다가 오랜 침잠에서 깨어나 스스로 빛을 발하듯, 갇힌 일상이나 현재를 억압하는 기억 속을 유영하다 어느 순간 현실로 솟구치는 인물들이기도 하다.

김양선(문학평론가)

The date plum, which grows leaves and bears fruit whether anyone cares or not, is a reminder that the plain and downtrodden also have their own lives to live and this fact is in itself brilliant and beautiful. Jeong Ji-a's characters also lead lives as insignificant as those of date plums, but have forged an ethical standard of living that comes from years of hardship. Like fish in the deep ocean floor with its "flat body and obsolete eyes cloaked in darkness" waking up from a long period of obscurity and becoming its own light, they float within the confines of their routines or the memories that oppresses the present and then suddenly make the leap into reality.

Kim Yang-seon(Literary critic)

K-픽션 026
검은 방

2020년 1월 30일 초판 1쇄 발행
2023년 6월 15일 초판 3쇄 발행

지은이 정지아 | 옮긴이 손정인 | 펴낸이 김재범
기획위원 전성태, 정은경, 이경재, 강영숙
편집 강민영, 김지연 | 관리 홍희표, 박수연 | 디자인 나루기획
인쇄·제책 굿에그커뮤니케이션 | 종이 한솔PNS
펴낸곳 (주)아시아 | 출판등록 2006년 1월 27일 제406-2006-000004호
주소 경기도 파주시 회동길 445
전화 031.944.5058 | 팩스 070.7611.2505 | 전자우편 bookasia@hanmail.net
ISBN 979-11-5662-173-7(set) | 979-11-5662-425-7 (04810)
값은 뒤표지에 있습니다.

K-Fiction 026
The Black Room

Written by Jeong Ji-a | **Translated by** Sohn Jung-in
Published by ASIA Publishers
Address 445, Hoedong-gil, Paju-si, Gyeonggi-do, Korea
Tel.(8231).944.5058 | **E-mail** bookasia@hanmail.net
First published in Korea by ASIA Publishers 2020
ISBN 979-11-5662-173-7(set) | 979-11-5662-425-7 (04810)